Amazon Story Bones

Also by Ellen Frye

Fiction

The Other Sappho

Look Under the Hawthorn

Nonfiction

The Marble Threshing Floor: A Collection of Greek Folk Songs

AMAZON STORY BONES

by
Ellen Frye

spinsters ink
minneapolis

Spinsters Ink
P. O. Box 300170
Minneapolis, MN 55403-5170

Cover art and design: Teri Talley

Production

Melanie Cockrell, Lynette D'Amico, Joan Drury, Cynthia Fogard, Kelly Kager, Lori Loughney, Rhonda Lundquist, Lou Ann Matossian, Lisa Schultz, Stefanie Shiffler, Liz Tufte

Library of Congress Cataloging-in-Publication Data
Frye, Ellen, 1940–
Amazon story bones / by Ellen Frye.
p. cm.
ISBN 1-883523-00-1 (paperback)
1-883523-01-X (hardcover)
1. Women soldiers—Greece—Mythology—Fiction.
2. Amazons—Mythology—Fiction. 3. Mythology, Greek—Fiction. I. Title.
PS3556.R9A47 1994
813'.54—dc20

93-41001
CIP

Printed in the U.S.A. on recycled paper with soy ink.

for Amazons, then and now

Acknowledgments

A number of the myths and tales first appeared (some in slightly different versions) in the journals and anthologies listed on the copyright page; I am grateful to the editors of those publications for their support.

I am also grateful to readers who commented on my work at different stages, including Amanda Powell, Athena Andreadis, Diane Edington, Ellin Sarot, Irene Zahava, Libby Oughton, Marcie Pleasants, Pamela Mittlefehldt, Patricia Roth Schwartz, Stephanie Smith, Susan Stinson, and Ursula Le Guin. Special thanks to Ellin Sarot for copy editing.

Scattered through the text are my own translations of modern Greek folk songs. I have also borrowed liberally from the endnotes of Robert Graves's *Greek Myths,* Volumes 1 and 2.

Re-vision—the act of looking back, of seeing with fresh eyes, of entering an old text from a new critical direction—is for women more than a chapter in cultural history: it is an act of survival.

—Adrienne Rich, *On Lies, Secrets, and Silence*

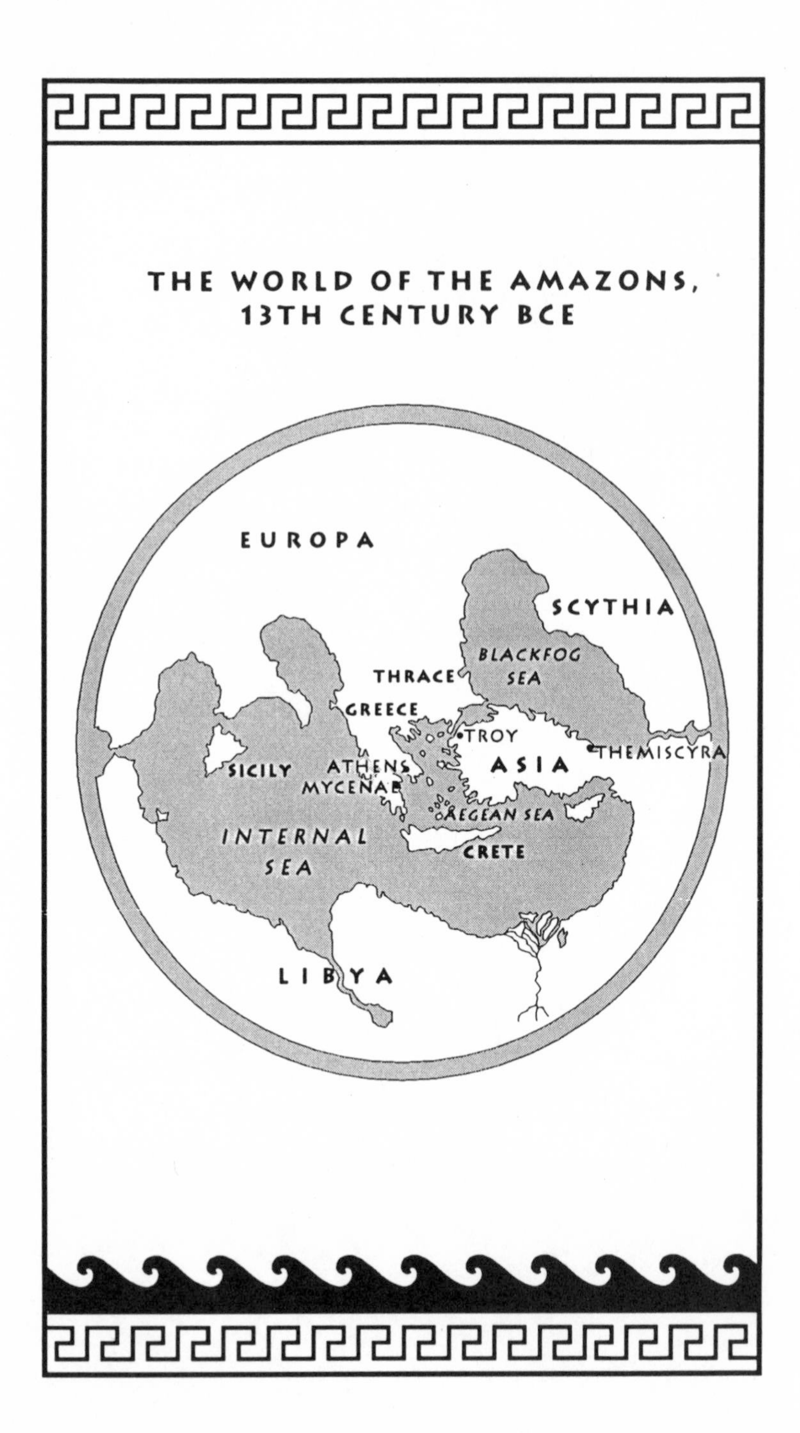
THE WORLD OF THE AMAZONS,
13TH CENTURY BCE
EUROPA
SCYTHIA
BLACKFOG SEA
THRACE
GREECE
TROY
THEMISCYRA
ASIA
SICILY
ATHENS
MYCENAE
AEGEAN SEA
INTERNAL SEA
CRETE
LIBYA

Prologue

Who were the Amazons?

Believe the ancient Greeks and you'll think they were single-breasted man-killers with long faces who mated randomly with strangers, maimed or killed their male progeny and suckled their daughters with mares' milk. It was the right breast they cut off, the better to draw a bow.

The men who wrote about the Amazons—and they *were* men, every one of them—knew nothing first-hand, yet they knew what they knew and they wrote it down. The Amazons did not write. Who holds the pen shapes history. With the stroke of a stylus, tittle-tattle becomes reality.

So the Greeks tell us the Amazons ruled themselves with queens, queens who all came to mean ends. One was dispatched by the Greek hero Heracles who took home as trophy her gold-spun warrior's belt. Another, abducted by the Athenian prince Theseus, fell in love with her rapist and betrayed her sisters when they came to rescue her. Another lost her honor and her life in the Trojan War. Unnatural women all, each deserved her comeuppance.

But what if the Amazons had carved their own myths in clay? What if they told their own stories? Imagine, if you will, a Homer singing the heroism of women...at her side a scribe recording the battle of Troy the Amazons knew.

Imagine then a mountain cave in Thrace, thirty-five years after Troy's last ember has grown cold. Two old women fuel the hearthfire with their stories. One speaks, one sings, and the winter air is peopled with women. A child stands at the cave wall drawing in charcoal...or sits by the fire with a clay tablet and a kingfisher's wing-feather.

The world turns; millenia pass. Outside, the cave entrance is blocked by a boulder; inside, animal bones.

If you could climb that Thracian mountain and push aside the boulder, you might find walls covered with script, charred tablets broken but readable. Deciphered, the marks might give voice to Amazons, the dry bones stand up and speak.

If bones did tell tales, these would not be ones you read in Greek mythology or *The Iliad*—no Zeus ruling the universe from Olympus, no heroes on the Trojan battle-field. Instead you might hear...stories of women telling stories of women.

A tale told by a woman is a bundle of threads. Lives ravel, unravel, ravel again. As you wind the threads onto the shuttle, don't fret over the missing bits. Threads of your own may belong in the weave.

And if you never read Greek mythology the way the men wrote it, so much the better. All you really need to know is that once upon a time Amazons lived on the Black Sea coast. For the rest, roll the unfamiliar names over your tongue and decide for yourself if they're tangy or sweet.

Open the bundle, take out a tale. Amazons ride the night air.

Mythological and Historical Characters

AEOLUS	god of winds
ANTIOPE	early Amazon leader, sister of Hippolyte
APHRODITE	goddess of love
APOLLO	god of arts
ARACHNE	spinner and weaver of sunset and dawn
ATHENA	goddess of wisdom and war
CASSANDRA	Trojan princess
CHIMERA	lion-headed creature with a goat's body and a snake's tail
CLEITE	Amazon leader, mother of Penthesilea
HERACLES	son of Zeus and latter-day Greek hero
HIPPOLYTE	early Amazon leader, sister of Antiope
MARPESSA	Trojan slave, companion to Cassandra
MEDUSA	gorgon, mother of Pegasus
PARIS	Trojan prince
PARTHENA	Trojan slave, wet nurse to Cassandra, mother of Marpessa
PEGASUS	flying horse, son of Medusa
PENTHESILEA	Amazon leader at time of Trojan War
POSEIDON	latter-day god of seas
THESEUS	prince of Athens and latter-day Greek hero
THETIS	mother goddess of Amazons
ZEUS	latter-day father god

MYTHS

Air gives breath to Amazon myths. Wind-blown from Scythia, carried on sea fog to a southern shore, they tell generations of Amazons who they are. Later, when Troy is a living memory, fragments will rise with the smoke in a Thracian cave. A child will gather the pieces and sing them down centuries to tell us who we were.

Thetis

the eastern Aegean
before the recording of time

Off the coast where Troy once stood, the long shadow of a mainland mountain fingers an island, an endless swell beats a rhythm against a cliff. Deep under the waves, sea horses ride the currents, limpets cling to rocks. The water is green and clear. It is the home of Thetis.

One noontide, as she tended a cuttlefish whose mother had gone up in a net, a surge of sea nymphs, fins fluttering, rolled into the grotto. "Mama Thetis!" they cried. "There's a stranger in the sea!"

"Muscles bulge out of its arms," said a bluenose, "but its paps are only pimples!"

Thetis tucked the cuttlefish into its cave. "Bulging arms, you say, and pimples on its chest." She rolled her tail. "That, my daughters, is a nereus, a creature like ourselves, only male. We don't often see them around here. Where is this stranger?"

Bluenose dipped her fin. "We were playing tag in an ebbtide just off the coast of Greece," she said. "He chased us away. He said he's building a palace there and a stable for his horses. He lashed his tail and agitated the water so, you couldn't tell whether the tide was flowing north or south."

Thetis sighed. Another upstart god, no doubt. They were everywhere these days. Only last night she'd listened to complaints about a child who came down from a mountain calling himself Zeus and pronouncing himself father of all, sole master of the universe. Father of all, indeed! As if fatherhood had to do with the *work* of creation! What man ever carried life in his belly, shaping its growth and finally thrusting it into the world? Why, then, would anyone pay attention to a god who called himself father of the universe? "Well, daughters," she said, "I must see who this creature is and what he wants." She swished her tail and plunged into a westbound undertow.

She found the nereus waving a trident, roaring at a battalion of dogfish.

"Put your weight to that seagreen boulder and set it here for the cornerstone! Wall up that gaping cavemouth! Lay the lower foundation along this ledge! Pull to it! I'll have this palace built before Zeus is half-done with Olympus."

Thetis settled herself on a rock in front of the cave marked for destruction. A hundred bass fry schooled around her, and a dog-headed, flipper-handed child of the sea jumped onto her lap.

"Bless you for coming," it whispered. "This crazy threatens us all. He wants to build a palace but he doesn't know anything about the sea. He ignores the rock castle that's already here—and all of us, for that matter. Last night I tried to tell him he was welcome to share our grotto, but he whipped his tail and I sailed halfway to Egypt. If I hadn't caught a ride with a dolphin, I'd be swimming back yet. Do talk to him. But goodness, be careful. He's got a terrible temper."

Thetis broke off a willow shoot and waved it. Churned-up silt drifted back to the sea floor. Fifty dogfish metamorphosed into finny statues. A jaw froze around an unroared bellow.

"It won't do to upset the denizens this way, you know," Thetis began. "I built this grotto myself. It was, I thought, a divine place to rest after I created the sea. It has served as castle to many a consort; surely it will serve you as well." She pointed the willow tip downward.

The frozen bellow formed an angry O under rapidly narrowing eyes. "*You* created this grotto, you say? And the rest of the *sea*?" The nereus moved closer.

"Of course. The sea and all its creatures." Thetis smiled. "All shore creatures as well, since they began in the sea. I am the moon who draws the sea to and from its land boundaries. I am Thetis. And you?"

The nereus navigated to the rock opposite. "*I* am Poseidon. My brothers and I are bound to put order into this universe. We drew lots yesterday, and I got the sea. Zeus got the sky. He thinks he's clever, always getting his way, but I'm going to build a palace that will show him the sea is as mighty as the sky." He cocked his head. "Your rock castle is nice, of course, but a little old-fashioned. No marble pillars, no gilt doorhandles. I need a stable for my horses, too. No one has horses like my white racers—pure bronze hooves, manes of gold. Now that I rule the sea, I'm going to drive my chariot through the waves, and, when I do, storms will cease and monsters rise from the depths to pay me homage." He leaned an elbow on his trident. "I created the horse, you know, and invented the bridle to tame it." He shifted expectantly. Thetis gazed at him serenely. He cleared his throat. "Listen, looking at you perched over there, I had an idea. You're a goddess of the sea, yes? And now I'm god of the sea. Why don't we marry? We'll have a great wedding, ambrosia flowing like rivers into a tidal basin. I'll introduce you to Zeus and my other brother Hades. You'll want to meet my three sisters, too. You can womantalk with them while my brothers and I plot the course of humankind. What do you say?"

Thetis flipped her tail. What a blowfish! Created the horse, indeed. Invented the bridle. The daughters were right about these godlings. They think no one exists but themselves. When they finally *see* a creature that's been there all along, they think they created it—as if it came to exist only through their eyes. And marry, what on earth is that? A rehearsal before the coupling? With his brothers and sisters? Why would a goddess travel to her consort's home for such a ceremony? Strange notions and stranger customs, these godlings. Still, I've coupled with worse to people this brine.

"You know, do you not, what the oracle says: any son of mine will be greater than his father. Does that fit into plotting the course of humankind?"

Poseidon fiddled with his trident. Grandfather Uranus had had his balls cut off by *his* seven sons; father Cronus had been run through by Zeus's thunderbolt. He slid off the rock and scudded along the ocean floor. "Well, it's been a pleasure meeting you. I'm sure we'll see each other from time to time. I really must get back to my construction." He shook his trident. One by one his troops toppled like masts in a gale. Poseidon scratched his belly. The sea was new to him; he didn't know its magic yet. He turned back to Thetis, ready to humble himself and ask for a spellbreaker, but the rock was bare, the grotto behind it a field of rippling eelgrass.

Under the sickle moon, Thetis climbed onto a ledge. She stretched her long tailfin and felt it divide. Scales melted into skin. Before the ledge was dry, her silver feet were running inland. It will take more than frozen dogfish to stop this godling, she thought. The grotto is safe for now, but as soon as the mist wears off, they'll be tearing things up again. Let me see if my moon priestesses can help.

By the time the sun had risen hot over the plain, she could feel the weight of change in the air. The road was wider than she remembered; iron-wheeled chariots thundered past her, charioteers whipping their horses to lightning speeds. Withered barley heads drooped on stalks in the fields; wide riverbeds held trickles of water. She stopped once to help an old woman fend wild dogs off her milch cow. On her way through a dark forest, she came upon a many-antlered deer dead from a boar's goring; nearby the boar nosed the trampled bush for berries.

The temple was tucked into a thicket of black poplar and cypress at the side of the sea. Branches twisted around the stone roof as if holding it from harm; sea-crows chattered on its dome. Thetis paused to admire the graceful sway of the fifty moon priestesses as they glided out of the temple and into a circle, each one bearing a clay vessel painted red and yellow and black. Water seeping through holes in the swinging vessels made damp spirals on the stone dancing floor.

Strange to pray for rain under the afternoon sun, thought Thetis. Even in this sacred place things do not go unchanged. She stepped out of the shadows to greet her daughters...but stopped as another robed figure emerged from the temple. Taller than the others, broader of shoulder, narrower of hip—a man. He leapt onto the sacred platform and into the center of the circle. The priestesses chanted and sprinkled their rainmakers around him. He raised his arms to the sun and, with a deep voice, called over the chant to the thunderer Zeus.

It's worse than I imagined, thought Thetis. My moon priestesses let a man invoke this godling for rain. She waited while the chant faded into hot, dry air. The priest, first to see her, ran and knelt at her feet.

"Mother goddess," he exclaimed, "you honor us. Are you pleased with how we weave your ancient wisdom into the bright dawn of our new age? Do you like our dance?"

Thetis looked up at the cloudless sky and back at the kneeling priest. The priestesses pressed close to her, waiting for her answer. She looked hard at each of them but could see no shame in a single eye.

"Much indeed has changed," she said finally. "And much, I confess, puzzles me. Who are you, young man? Why do you pray to the sun for rain?"

The young man's smile floated in charm. "Well, as you can see, we have changed none of the rituals of the night. We only enhance them by adding the sun's brilliance to the moon's soft glow. I am winner of the foot race in the last Great Year. I thought how better to be lover to these fifty maidens than to enrobe myself and join their dance. Everyone agrees the ceremonial enhancements I suggest make our rites richer, more likely to gain our desires."

Such as rain for parched barley. Thetis frowned. If I send them rain this night, they'll think it comes from their new godling and the godling will believe it comes from his own power. If I don't, the crop will fail, children will starve, and they'll blame the old ways. Perhaps it's time for me to travel abroad, to see how widespread is this invasion of the spirit.

Silver-finned again, Thetis rode the waves out from the Greek shore, closing her ears to the booms reverberating from the depths of the sea. East through the Aegean she sailed, until she reached the calm waters that lay between Lesbos and the shadow of Mount Ida on the mainland. Moonbeams splashed the night waves, and a gentle wind rippled her fins. Thetis closed her eyes and rolled. Mmmm, how I've missed these soft Aeolian breezes, she thought. Soft, yet strong, making my nipples stand up. She opened her eyes to Aeolus, whose salty breaths were ruffling her skin. "How nice to see a god of my own generation. You've no idea what the youngbloods are doing in the western isles."

The wind god laughed. "So I've heard. You're wise to come this way. People here are seafarers; they know who pulls the sea. All through Anatolia, your temples stand under a timeless sky." The cry of a kingfisher drifted across the night water. "Listen," he whispered. "She's building her thorny nest to float on the waves. Tonight is the longest night of the year. Dear goddess of all things, shall we join her in creating new life? My winds will not ruffle the sea for seven days, and this world needs more of your children. Perhaps your belly will swell with a new tribe who can make our eastern lands safe from the spread of the warrior gods."

Thetis rolled under a wave and dove deep. When she surfaced, her head was cone-shaped and crowned with seaweed. Eight snaky arms reached out from her shell, at the end of each arm a coral-toothed mouth. Aeolus laughed and sent eight zephyrs to tickle each tentacle and one to kiss the green head.

"You think I don't find your cuttlefish guise beautiful?" he said. "I have loved you in every shape you've ever dreamed. I loved you when I still floated in your watery womb. I watched you breathe life into drops of brine. They wriggled around you, and you let them find their own way into fins and scales, blubbery hides, crusts smooth or spiny. You gave each of us what we needed to go our own way. Myself, I wanted to be a thing that could touch you always, so when you divided the sea from the sky and set the universe in motion, I learned how to turn and twist over you, to roar and to be gentle. Now I've a whole bagful of winds to carry me—gusts and blasts and gales, zephyrs and puffs and whiffs."

Thetis, floating, let her snaky arms radiate around her. "I love to hear my story in your voice. Tell me how it seemed to you when green mountains rose out of my depths."

Aeolus cut a series of loops and sent a dozen mare's tails scuttling across the moon. "They looked like lumpy monsters floating on the waves. I watched them spread wide and welcome the creatures that crawled out of the water. I breathed into the gills of the newly landed ones. They liked that and said goodbye to their sisters and brothers of the sea. And you—you came landward, too. Or at least a part of you. The upright creatures in these parts call you Cybele; other places they call you Bendis... Rhea...Hecate. You have as many names as you have shapes. And I, dear goddess of life-in-death, of death-in-life, have loved them all." Aeolus spun until a spout of water lifted the divine cuttlefish toward the stars and set her back gently onto the foam.

The eight tentacles stretched until each was a creature alone. Thetis, herself again, laughed. "You're right. It's time to hatch a new race. Yes, my son and first consort, I need not dance lonely on the waves. Blow your winds into me gentle and strong. But, remember, only for seven days."

Coming into her time, Thetis sought a place perfect for the new race. She left the sheer cliffs of Anatolia behind her and turned toward the northernmost corner of the Aegean. They'll need mountains and plains, she thought, and a fast rushing river. I think I'll make them horse-lovers. But no chariots; they'll ride astride, one with their beasts. She skimmed through a channel. Thrace loomed to her left, Anatolia to her right. Not here, she thought, nor there. Too close. They'll need a place far enough from those unruly and ignorant godlings so that they can grow strong in themselves.

The Blackfog Sea, shrouded in mist, opened before her. On the farther shore, the Scythian steppe rolled with wormwood and vetch.

Out of the water, she let her silver fintail grow into long and sinewy legs, her arms stretch to match them. Crescent hooves tipped all four, and her neck arched gracefully under a silver mane. How better to birth horse-lovers than from a mare, she thought, as she carried her swollen belly toward a great white oak. Grey dawn, reflected from the pool next to it, turned rosy.

The foal came easily, black all over. Spindly black legs, shiny black body, black face, black eyes, black mane, black tail. Black is the beginning of this race, thought Thetis, as the foal lips closed over a teat. The filly stopped sucking and nickered. Thetis spun the earth and made her a yearling.

"Well, my daughter," she said, "I leave you now. Next year, you'll lose your hooves and take on a woman's shape. You'll be twenty-one in human years. A man-creature will appear from the north. Consort with him, then leave him. Find a cave that faces the rising sun. Light a fire of laurel, and wait for your time to come. You'll bear twins. The seasons will turn, and your twins will bear twins, your twins' twins will bear twins. You'll call yourselves Amazons, and you'll live apart from your children's fathers. You will count yourselves only by the mother." The filly pawed the brown earth, withers rippling. Thetis continued her instructions. "Each time you bear children, you'll suckle the boys a full turning of the sun; then you'll crown their heads with ivy and carry them to their waiting fathers. The girls you'll keep with you, and you'll raise them healthy, strong and heroic."

The filly kicked her heels. Thetis trotted to the shore. Hooves melted into scales as she dove into the sea.

"Take care, little one," she called from a wave. "You can find me wherever foam kisses the shore. Or, if you're far from the sea, look for me in the moon. I'm there, too. Ride well...and remember the mother."

Pegasus

a mountain in Anatolia
a flying horse

Time was when Dawn greeted morning on a winged horse, a proud beast, as much thunderer in air as on earth. When Dawn finished painting the tangled wormwoods of our steppe, she folded his feathers into his withers and dropped him gently to earth.

His name was Pegasus—Springforth—because he had sprung, fully formed, from the decapitated head of his mother Medusa. She was one of our sisters of the sea, a silver-scaled gorgon with a crown of undulating serpents. A mad Greek slew her, affronted by her eyes that turned away intruders by making of them stone things. Her story is another story. His story is that his first look on this world was his mother's death.

He made his home on Chimera, a mountain to the south of here that, from time to time, breathes fire. Mornings he roamed its foot, talking with the serpents of the marsh; midday he cavorted with the goats in the higher meadows; he took his nightly rest with the lions who ranged the desolate crater of the peak. His magic was not that he could fly—any winged creature could fly—but that a single hoof-strike could create a spring of burbling water. When the dry years came and the lions lay panting for rain, he made his way from pride to pride planting moon-shaped waterholes.

One morning Thunder chased Dawn, and Pegasus drifted early to earth, far from his mountain. He took shelter under a willow and, when the sun finally shattered the black clouds, trotted out into a lush, dripping countryside. Vineyards stepped up the hillsides, laurels blossomed along a river bank. He ambled upstream, watching the river run. The closer the sun climbed toward noon, the faster the water raced. At the moment of the sun's overhead pause, Pegasus arrived at a waterfall, sheer rock down which the river tumbled. Waist-deep in the pool at the foot of the falls, a man stood singing:

My name is Killer of Bellerus,
and I've come to slay the dragoness.
The lion of her I'll smash with my club,
her goat's back I'll riddle with arrows.
Then I'll snatch her snaketail and swing her around
and fling her over the moon.

Even motherless, Pegasus was mannered. He greeted the Greek.

"Good noontide. May I drink from your water?"

"If you don't mind a little piss, drink as you like." The Greek shook water from one ear and the other. Then he pounded his chest and sloshed to the bank.

"Eyaaah!" A war whoop rang off the rock.

Pegasus lifted his muzzle in time to see a sword slice a greensnake in two. He stared as the Greek picked up the head and threw it against the rock. The tail writhed on the bank. The splotch on the rock grew into his mother's face.

"Seven by noon!" crowed the Greek. "You've brought me luck, friend. Seven times seven and twice again seven means the monster will fall and the king's daughter be mine. I thank you for your assistance."

Pegasus pulled himself away from his mother's shadow. He looked at the Greek who hunkered skinning the tail. Bent over the pool, an elderberry held a sword belt dangling six more. Pegasus found his voice and asked, "What could I do to persuade you to stop at seven? What will the king take in lieu of seven times seven and twice again seven?"

The Greek looked up from his work and eyed Pegasus. "You don't like dead snakes?" he asked. "What are dead snakes to a stallion like you?" Pegasus stood as still as his trembling muscles let him. "Well," continued the Greek, "do you know where the monstrous chimera lives? The one with a lion's head, a goat's body and, fegh! a slimy snake for a tail? Help me destroy her. I'm weakening her with every snake I kill, but with your power under me, I could take her down now. What do you say?"

Pegasus knew that his own mountain was named for the creature and that she lived in a cave at the rim of the crater. She rarely ventured out these days, staying inside for years at a time, tending her sacral fires. As a child, hungry somehow for the maternal touch he'd never known, he had often buried his head deep in her mane and listened to the solid thud of her heart. She was the one who taught him the turning of the year—where to forage in winter, where the first buds blossomed, which trees were shelter from the fierce summer sun. From time to time, when a storm left him shank-deep in drifts, she would make her teats swell and let him suckle.

Pegasus looked at the Greek who had strapped on his

swordbelt and stood stroking his seven skins. Would the man know the chimera from a decoy? The deal was struck. "But," said Pegasus, "not today. If we go tomorrow, I'll have wings to fly you. Only Dawn can unfold them, so tomorrow I'll tell her to leave them spread and I'll meet you here as soon as the plain turns amber."

Midnight found the mountain animals carving. A lion's head grew from butternut, a chunk of birch gave way to goat. Shed hair was gathered for the mane. Leaves matted with mud made ears.

"The tail must wave to attract his attention," said Pegasus. "Who will brave the Greek's arrows?"

A water moccasin raised its flat head. "I can dart my tongue to the four winds and never move my tail. The Greek's arrows won't touch me."

The animals danced until Dawn slipped among them and climbed into her saddle. As morning pink melted to gold, Pegasus floated down to the waterfall. The Greek was waiting as if for war. Greaves, cuirass and helmet left no more than a pair of eyes to the elements. All along the river bank, an arsenal gleamed.

"Sword, I'll need both broad and long," the Greek was muttering, "and the dagger with the emerald shaft, I don't want to leave that behind. A battle ax for hacking, and, here, I'll take this ashwood spear. And both javelins, and my short thrusting spear. Now for the bow. The bighorn, of course, but I'd best take a short one, too. Yes, and my slingshot." He glanced up at Pegasus. "There you are. Look at this. A bullet of pure lead. When I sling it into her fiery maw, it will melt down her throat and sizzle her innards."

He thrust a twisted bronze bit into Pegasus' mouth. Pegasus started. "Whoa," cried the Greek. "A deal's a deal. Steady now." Pegasus accepted the shackle and stood still while a saddle was bound to his back. The Greek hoisted the weapons onto the saddle and clanked up after them.

Pegasus took the long way around, not to let the Greek know how close Mount Chimera was to the waterfall. He flew through the mists guarding the Blackfog Sea and circled three times over our wormwood steppe. He took the Greek across five rivers, along the coast of the Aegean and over the great walls of Troy. The Greek fondled his weapons and told tales of his previous ordeals.

"I'm not from around here, you know," he called above the rush of wind. "I'm from a city called Corinth, famous for wine and brave men. I killed someone there; he wanted a handsome dagger of mine, and I gave it to him in his belly. It turned out he was the royal barber. The king exiled me to the coast, a miserable place, I thought, until I saw the coast king's daughter. She had eyes for me, too, I could tell by the way she averted her face every time she saw me. Oh, she wanted me, all right. She resisted, of course–what woman doesn't? They all cry, 'No, no,' wanting every inch of it. I took her hard, and she loved it." The Greek spat into a cloud. "Then the bitch cried rape, and her father sent me packing. So I came to these shores. Beautiful princess here, too, but her father keeps her locked in a tower. He says I can have her, anyone can have her who kills the dreadful chimera. Well, I say to myself, I'm handsome and I'm strong. I've got swords for fighting and a ramrod for loving. I can give the old man grandbabies enough to make a dozen kingdoms flourish. He's lucky I even want her.... Hey, is that the demon's lair? I'm itching for action!"

Mount Chimera ranged before them, bright with sunshine. Out of the crater spiraled a single plume, a reminder of the violence a mountain can make. The decoy lay on a flat rock as if sunning itself. The moccasin saw them and waved.

"There she is, the bitch! Here's a spear to her festering eye and a leadball for her filthy mouth. Hey, circle round again and let me draw my bow on her." A dozen arrows sprouted from the decoy's back. The moccasin danced and waved and held on tight. On the third pass, the Greek leaned over and lopped off an ear. "There! Proof of my prowess. The king will know what a warrior I am!"

Pegasus kicked his heels and beat his wings upward. Enough, he thought, and flew into a cloud. Just before the mist covered him, he looked back. The single plume was a billow, the flat rock broken in two. The sullen rumbling he had heard throughout the Greek's display erupted into a roar. The mountain burst into fire.

Pegasus flew the roundabout journey in reverse, sprinkling tears over Troy, the Aegean and the Blackfog Sea. When he came to our wormwood steppe, he looked down and saw our Amazon warriors gathered for a gaming. A hare was running, a sister hard on its heels. Pegasus circled to watch the chase. The hare scrambled into a gully: the harechaser leapt and charged down the other side. The hare cut through a briar patch: the chaser careened over it and waited. The chase was so fine, Pegasus forgot the burden on his back. An arrow past his nose reminded him. He snorted and started to climb out of range, but found his head held down, the twisted bit crushing tongue into teeth. "Stay low," snarled the Greek. "Why waste arrows? Women on horseback, fegh! I can take the lot of them. When I'm done, you'll fly me straight to Zeus. I'm due a hero's reward!"

The Amazons were slow to take up their weapons. Flying over them, after all, was Pegasus, Pegasus who brought them each new day, whose hooves had given them running water. Even when they understood that

Pegasus was bound by a foreign bridle, they were reluctant to pick up their bows. What if an arrow dug into horseflesh? The harechaser found the way. She ran to a gnarled wormwood, home to a queenless hive. "Honey is sweet," she called into the air, "but the bee stings!" Wrapped in honeycomb, her arrow flew upward, a swarm of angry drones following. When the arrow fell short, the bees flew on. A sting on Pegasus' nose made him sneeze out the wretched bit; another on his flank, and the saddle flew off. The Greek fell, lances, daggers, and bows tumbling after him. He landed in the briar patch. The Amazons, games spoiled, left him there cursing. Pegasus, unburdened, flew homeward.

The smoking mountain could be seen all the way to the sea. Pegasus touched down at its foot where cypress trees trembled knee-deep in marshwater. A giant old one had given up its rootedness and lay full-length across the swamp. The snakes were mourning the moccasin who had been killed after all, not by a Greek arrow but by flying rock. The goats were there, too, in retreat from their rumbling meadows. The lions had come down from the crater.

"The chimera," asked Pegasus, "is she still in her cave?"

"We called and called," said an old lion. "When her lintelstone fell, we left. Go to her, Pegasus. She'll listen to you. Ask her to calm the mother's anger."

The cave entrance was rubble. Pegasus remembered another way in, a passage that slanted into a lower chamber. He found the chimera waiting for him and buried his head in her mane. Her heartbeat rang solid through his bones. Over their heads, the mountain raged. Time passed. The fury dwindled. Then silence.

"I didn't mean to make her angry," he cried. "He was killing snakes. To weaken you, he said. I thought if I could send him away with what he thought he wanted, the least harm would be done."

The chimera pushed him until they could lock eyes. "You do what you do out of what you know. Now the mother has given you another design. When you are outraged, rage out. When you are offended, be so. A cloak of skin wears well with friends, but know when to put on mail." The chimera guided him to the front entrance. The lintel was back in place. A fresh wind nibbled the billows. Sunshine poked at grey ash. "Go," she said, "your friends are rebuilding their nests. Your strong back may be of use."

Medusa

an island off Libya
three sisters and a boy

Once, three sisters lived on an island. Home was a cave on an eastern cape, a willow grove where a spring ebbed when the tide was flooding and flowed when the tide ran out. The island was bare rock and deep forest and pastureland so rich the cows gave curds instead of milk.

The sisters were gorgons, and they called themselves Stronger, Roamer, and Medusa. Roamer hunted the forest on legs long and narrow as a mare's. Stronger worked the loam with a back as wide as a valley. Medusa herded the cattle and sang. Her faced glowed like a harvest moon—except when she was angry. Then her eyes flared into burning coals, fangs pushed over her lips, and her curls writhed like snakes. Her shoulder blades sprouted wings, and her brazen hands curled into claws. She would stick out her tongue and hiss until the unlucky intruder stood stone-still and breathless. By the time Medusa had breasts the size of crab apples, a dozen or more stunned rocks lined the river that ran out of the spring and into the sea.

Every year, when the willows petaled the river in yellow and trumpeting cranes cut the sky, the sisters counted the sun's diminishing and looked for the arrival of the three grey ones, sisters, cousins of the gorgons. Neither old nor young, only grey, they shared a single eye. Whoever had the urge to see planted the eye on her forehead and led the others. A single tooth was theirs, too, and on the trail they traded eye for tooth and tooth for a crane-feathered pouch. The pouch contained bones. It was the bones the gorgons waited for.

When yearly the grey ones hobbled into the grove, every willow had to be surveyed thrice by the single eye, thrice probed by the single tooth. Long after the sun had purpled the west and disappeared, the grey ones traded eye for tooth, tooth for pouch, and eye for tooth again. The gorgons watched them and waited until finally the drawstring was loosened and the bones spilled into the moonlight. One last swap of eye for tooth, and then the stories began.

"Now here," the one with the eye would begin, poking two curved sow's ribs around the wing bone of a raven, "here she became a dove and brooded on the waves. The egg she laid floated seven aeons. Then her serpent son embraced it till it cracked. Out came sun and moon, stars and planets, mountains, rivers, and trees. The sea was no longer alone. Earth and sky were her companions." She nodded to Stronger who picked up the bones and hung them from the willow. Eye and tooth were passed.

The second grey one picked out three lion vertebrae and set them over a tailbone. "Here," she said, "is our canine guardian of the underworld. Her nightly duty is gathering asphodel to feed the spirits. Her mother is a sister of yours, you know her as well as we do. She lives underwater and eats fishermen raw. Do you remember when the Dog Star took a dive, how she fancied him? That's why your niece is three-headed: one from her father and two from her mother. All in the world makes sense, you see. Now, the aconite you plaster to bring down a swelling grows wherever the hellhound slavers. So does henbane, but you must be careful of that one: too strong it makes you dizzy, too weak it drives you mad." She sat back on her heels, and Roamer hung the triple doghead from a limb. Eye and tooth were passed again.

"Now here," said the third grey one, setting a falcon's breastbone over seven dog dewclaws, "here is a fine foremother of ours. Sow of plenty, she dives into the chasms and helps spirits leave their bodies. Eats them right up, the bodies, and sprouts corn. When the north wind blows, the plain fills with seedlings. Yours, Medusa, to hang."

One year, in the middle of the tale of the hydra whose seven severed heads each grew seven more, a barque glided onto the river, turned smartly into the wind, and, sails flapping, fetched to an extended willow root. Medusa swiveled her head. Wings sprouted from her shoulder blades, and her tongue darted out. The barque trembled.

"Wait, sister!" cried Stronger. "Look, no hand holds the steering oar. Before you turn it to stone, let's see how it sails itself."

They approached the boat. Behind them the single eye vaulted from forehead to forehead, the tooth from mouth to mouth. The willows murmured.

The barque's steering oar, strapped to the after gunwale, swayed in the water. Midship, a naked baby played with his toes.

"See there, sister," said Roamer, "would you petrify a harmless child?" She pulled the barque along the bank. The baby cooed. Medusa's tongue darted, yet around it her mouth curled in a smile. She reached out to touch the downy head, then stepped into the barque and hefted the infant. Could an innocent be an intruder?

The sisters hurried through the grove to show their treasure to the grey ones, but at the storytree, they found the grey ones had vanished. No sign of them in the grove or on the river trail or as far as the eye could see across pastureland.

"Look, they left us the pouch," said Roamer. "Perhaps they mean it's time we told the stories ourselves. Here, let me cradle our Precious. It's your turn, Medusa, to hang sister Hydra from the tree."

The grey ones never returned. The infant toddled, the toddler ran. Rainy days, his smile brought them sunshine; snowbound, they heard spring in his laughter. He grew straight as a cypress. When he asked for a ball to play with, Roamer strode to the setting sun to bring back the golden apple from the far western orchard. The winter he fevered, Stronger crossed ice and snow to find a cure of hare's cheese and wild goat's milk. One day he stood taller than any of them, and he asked for a flying horse. Medusa, whose eyes had burned not once since his coming and whose tongue had forgotten the shape of a hiss, jumped into the river. "I'm off to the Aegean," she called. "A new seagod has built a palace off the coast of Greece. He has a stable full of horses and surely one of them can fly."

She found the stable but none of the horses had wings. The seagod, though, had eyes that coveted her.

"Poseidon, at your service. You admire my horses, I see. They're the finest bred. You must come and watch them draw my chariot over and under the waves. The fish stop swimming, and the monsters of the deep rise up to pay me homage. And you, my dear, what can I do for you?"

"I'm looking for a horse with wings, one that can canter under and over the waves and also fly to the moon."

"Well," said Poseidon, "I've no need to fly. The sky's my brother's territory, and, anyway, I've enough to do keeping the sea in order. But"—he let his arm drape lightly across her shoulders—"perhaps together we might make a flying horse. You're broad of thigh and sweet of face, and your shoulder blades, I see, can wing themselves. There's a quaint grotto behind my palace. It belonged to a sea nymph once and, out of respect for her, I've kept it as she made it. It's a lovely place to lie. Come with me?"

Medusa mused. Why not? Mama Thetis foaled the first Amazon. Why shouldn't I carry a colt to delight the boy of our grove?

Medusa swam back to the island and found her sisters moping. "He's gone away," said Stronger. "He sailed right after you left. He said he wanted gear for his horse and he knew where to find it. We begged him to wait, but he turned his back to us."

"Well," laughed Medusa, "he'll have to come home. I'm carrying his horse in my belly." She jumped out of the river and rolled onto her back. Overhead a V of cranes straggled across the sky. "Look!" she cried. "It's almost time for the stories. Don't worry, sisters, he'll be back. He loves the bones as much as we do."

The days shrank. Finally the sisters saw their Precious sailing on a flood tide, his barque filled with a bundle. He tied up to the willow root and tossed his bag onto the bank. The sisters stared. His face was no longer golden, and he wore a full red beard over his mouth. His eyes, still blue, glinted more pierce than sparkle.

"Well, aunties, greet me! I've been to see my people. Look what they've given me!" He pulled a helmet from his sack and set it over his ears. "Bronze," he said, "smelted by the finest. That's the plume of an ostrich on top; you should have heard her croak when I plucked it from her tail!" He rummaged. "My greaves—lion heads on the knees, see? Bronze to stop an arrow, but the lion heads are silver." He strapped them onto his shins. Then he pulled out a sword and whipped the air with it. "Look at me, aunties—am I not a warrior?"

The sisters' joy at his return was tempered with perplexity. "Why battle gear, son?" asked Medusa. "Is there a war somewhere that threatens us?"

"No war," shrugged Precious. "No war here at all. That's why I went away and why I'm going again. A man must prove himself a man." He cocked his head at them. "You know I love and respect you, aunties, but you're not my people. My people are over the sea. Greeks. I visited them for this gear. Now I go to seek my destiny." He hesitated, smiling. "With your permission, I'll take the bones with me. My people, I think, might find them valuable.

They might even trade gold for them." He reached toward the feathered pouch hanging from a branch. Medusa's hand was faster. "Oh, come now, auntie," he pouted. "You know those old stories by heart. No need to keep hanging them from trees."

Medusa held the pouch to her breast. Her eyes began to burn, and her hair curled into snakes. Precious stepped back. "All right," he said, still smiling. "I'll trade you for them." He spread his palm. A single tooth gleamed, a single eye glared up at her.

Shoulder blades into wings, nails into claws, Medusa felt a hiss rise in her throat. "No!" she cried, "I carry no horse for a plunderer." Fangs pushed over her lips.

"Hide your face, son!" Roamer still saw the boy beneath the helmet, the cooing mouth behind the beard. "Stop, Medusa! He's only playing. He doesn't mean to take the bones. He's our baby, our child!"

Medusa's tongue paused, the hiss still behind it. Precious took his advantage and plucked a shield from his battle gear. His face safe behind bronze, he swung his sword. Medusa's head, spewing hisses, sped skyward.

The willows tossed her hisses into the river. Fierce eddies kicked the rocks. From the airborne head a foal unfolded, legs first, then wings. By the time its hooves touched earth, it was a stallion, an Amazon on its back. Horse and warrior charged. Precious dove into the river, caught hold of his barque, and rushed with the current seaward.

The Amazon dismounted. "Grieve for your sister, a woman fierce and gentle." She lifted the pouch from Medusa's headless breast and handed it to Roamer. "A new story waits. Here. Search out the bones. Find the truth of it. Tell it. Hang it from the storytree."

Medusa's snake-crowned head flew over the gibbous moon. Roamer searched until she found three crane wing tips and a ferret's knucklebone. "Once," she began, "three sisters lived on an island...." Medusa's head inscribed an arc across the outer sky. By the time the bones were hung from the willow, Medusa had entered the cycle of heaven. You can see her high on a midwinter night. Watch closely. She pulses. Two days bright, she reminds us of the fire that forges strength. When she dims, we remember that fire also brings pain. Then she's bright again.

Hippolyte

Themiscyra, the Amazon city
the southern coast of the Blackfog Sea

Once, long after we left the Scythian plain and came to the opposite shore of the Blackfog Sea, two sisters led our warriors. Hippolyte, the elder, moved like a wind-touched willow; the younger Antiope saw the world through the eyes of a sparrow hawk. Home was a stone city that straddled a river. Upstream, the river watered a plain roany with mares, purple with vetch. Downstream it fell over rocks and poured into a cliff-ringed harbor. Beyond the cliffs, the sea rolled some days under forbidding mists, some days under a blue and beckoning sky.

One blue-sky day, the sisters and a child stood on the outermost cliff, leaning into the wind, watching a speck on a wave grow into a narrow, sailing galley. Closer, it cut through cross-waves and drove straight for the wall of rock, then turned abruptly, and, oars akimbo, careened through the gap and into the harbor's flat calm.

"Well sailed," remarked Hippolyte. "Not many can navigate our slip."

"But look at the eyes on the ram-beaked prow, mark the upsweeping stern." Antiope, the scholar, wary and rational, kept her voice low. "It's a Greek ship. Dangerous." She touched the head of the child beside her. "Quick, my pet, to the tower. Set the wooden clackards dancing. Let the archers know we are invaded."

The girl turned to run, but Hippolyte, rash as Antiope was cautious, caught her arm. "Hey," she said, "it's only a single-deck, not even a warship. The man at the steering oar, the one bellowing like a bull—see how the muscles roll under his hairy flesh? Our annual seed-gathering is not so far off. Why not use these strangers? Everyone wearies of the clumsy Gargarensians."

Antiope frowned. "Clumsy, sister, but known to us. Greeks are ruthless not only on the battlefield. When their pirate bands sack a city, they kill the men and ravage the women. What they do to children is too wicked to whisper." She tapped the girl again. "Go, pet." And back to Hippolyte. "Let her run. Their seed might give our tribes new muscle, but the risk is far too great."

Hippolyte, stubborn and fearless and attracted to danger, tossed a knotted rope over the edge of the cliff and lowered herself to the rocky shore. Around her waist, her golden warrior's belt, gift of the hundred-handed one, caught the morning's first sunlight and danced it back to the cliff. The Greek galley tilted under twenty oarsmen gaping at the rail.

"Well you have come into our harbor, stranger," she called to the sternsman. "I am Hippolyte, daughter of Zerinthia. What do you call yourself, and why have you journeyed here?"

The sternsman glared over the water. "I am Heracles, son of Zeus," he pronounced. "I subdued poison-fanged serpents while still a babe in my crib. At nine I lopped off the ears, eyes, and noses of every Minyan herald; at fifteen I tied the king of the Euboeans to two colts and set them running in opposite directions." He tossed his copper curls. "Those were my childish deeds."

Hippolyte raised an eyebrow. "You were indeed a brave boy," she said. "And you journey here for...?"

Heracles threw back his shoulders. "I have chosen as my future bride the daughter of a king, and I must accomplish twelve tasks before I wed her. I've already finished eight." He frowned and counted on his fingers. "I wrestled the Nemean lion; I severed the immortal heads of the Hydra; I ensnared the Erymanthian boar; I river-cleansed the Augean stables; I rattled into madness the Stymphalian birds; I captured the fire-breathing Cretan bull; I tamed the wild Thracian horses. Now I am to...." He eyed the golden belt around the Amazon waist. Hippolyte waited. "Now I am to fetch your golden girdle, your matchless warrior's belt. We'll fight for it, Hippolyte, queen of the Amazons, your choice of weapons against my olive club. If you win, I give you all the treasure in my ship's hold; if you lose, the belt is mine."

Hippolyte ran her finger along the crescent blade at her belt. She shrugged. "I accept. But before we fight, why don't you and your men come into our city for a feasting? We'll exchange gifts of honor. We'll dance to the rattling quivers' rhythm. If you like, we'll climb to the mating rock. You give us your seed, and we'll show you how we play." Heracles opened his mouth, but no words came. He looked at his saucer-eyed men and back at Hippolyte. She laughed. "Hey, stranger, are you up to it? Or shall I let my warriors' flaming arrows set your sails ablaze? A proposal wants an answer."

"Dunderheads!" he hissed at his drooling men. "Wipe the spittle from your beards! We are invited to carouse."

Hippolyte was already half-way up the cliff. Heracles and his men scrambled over the railing and thrashed through the water. At the shore, they found the headland empty; only the dangling rope gave them direction.

Clouds cut the rising moon. The dancers circled, crescent shields flashing. Heracles' men, lumped near the wine barrels, picked goat meat from their teeth and admired the bobbing breasts. The sudden sound of arrows rattling alerted them to a new rhythm. The dancers were moving away from the firelight. Eager for the promised mating, the men tossed their goblets aside and scrambled after them. Outside the city, the procession snaked along the river toward a mountain rising straight from the plain. The frenzied quiver-rattling drove dancers and followers up steps cut into the rocks. The path switched back once, twice, three times. Then the rhythms stopped.

Gathering clouds left the night char-black. Heracles and his men felt their way through a narrow rock-walled passage. Emerging onto a wide ledge, each man was grasped firmly by a pair of strong hands. Heracles tried to commandeer his senses, but his brain was thick. Insistent hands stroked him, pushed him down. Murmurs surrounded him. Despite the wine and the climb, his rod stiffened. An anonymous undulating tunnel sheathed it. Before he could collect himself, his seed had spurted and the sheath was gone. He peered into the starless night, but could see only darting shadows. He flung his hands along the cliff face searching for the passage out, but the wall of rock was seamless. His men, splayed over the ledge, began to snore.

At last, grey dawn cracked the eastern sky. A hawk cried. Heracles squinted down at the silent city and frowned.

Inside rough-hewn walls, the city was coming to life. Had you opened the stable doors, you would have seen bearskin-clad girls aiming streams of mare's milk into clay jugs, tots pulling brown-flecked eggs from under nested hens. Along the street that ran to the South Gate, a flaxen-headed child followed a band of nannies and rattled her herder's stick over cobbles. On the steps of the Great Hall, Hippolyte and Antiope were discussing the Greeks.

"What do you say to letting the broadmuscles win back their honor?" posed Hippolyte. "The big one, Heracles, wants to grapple with me singlehanded. Why not let them win a few rounds before I tackle him? You've studied their habits, sister. What do they do well, besides sacking cities?"

"Heracles is said to be a strong wrestler," mused Antiope. "He's good at club-bashing and wields the sword swiftly. He left his club, by the way, in the central square, next to the wine barrels. I hung it from the plane tree. I expect he'll be here soon to claim it."

Two giggling girls pushed each other up the steps.

"The funny-men are in the central square," cried one

of them, out of breath. “The big one’s yelling. He says you have to come right now.”

“I told her not to laugh, but she wouldn’t listen to me,” said the other.

“Well, she said he sounded like a wild sow defending her farrow. Of course I laughed.”

Hippolyte rested a hand on each child’s shoulder. “Well done,“ she said. “Let’s not keep our guest-strangers waiting.” She took Antiope’s arm. “Why don’t you round up the councillors? Plan an afternoon of contests with some dazzling trophies. They came all this way for a girdle, they mustn’t sail away empty-handed. Now, for my duel with Heracles, what do you advise?”

Antiope looked up at the cloudless, cornflower sky. “Let the children come with me,” she said. “I’ll need their legs for message-running. A pentathlon might be best. You could start with the clubs and a short-dagger duel. Then, a footrace around Mount Dirphis, with a pause at the eastern lookout to throw lances to Mount Hyrcania. Finish at the harbor with wrestling. Let it be a match that encourages their leave-taking yet holds their honor intact.”

Antiope hurried away, the children trotting beside her. Hippolyte strode toward the central square, enjoying her shadow leaping along the wall ahead of her.

The hills that rimmed the gaming field reddened with late afternoon sun. The Greeks fondled their newly-won greaves, their helmets, their emerald-studded axes.

Their eyes on the booty instead of breasts, they'd demonstrated a prowess that had pleased the Amazons and made the contests even-scored. Everyone waited for the final encounter.

Hippolyte, juggling five black-walnut clubs, selected the two most perfectly balanced and let three little girls catch the rejects. Antiope touched her arm.

"Our shore patrols have returned," she said. "They scouted two more ships anchored upcoast with men armed and waiting for a signal. The Greeks plan to sail into the harbor during the final match and surprise us. This Heracles is desperate for your warrior's belt."

Hippolyte fingered the golden threads, gift of the hundred-handed one. "Are the archers stationed already, or did you tell them to wait until the footrace begins?"

"Two contingents are in the woods, the rest here to swell the crowd. A horse and rider wait at the shore to carry word of the first movement. Fourteen archers are ready to loose flaming arrows before the galleys reach the slip."

Hippolyte smiled. "We're ready then. On with the match."

She stepped forward, and Amazons and Greeks formed a circle around the two contestants. Heracles' wild olive arced; one black walnut met it coming, the other glanced off its side. Heracles advanced, Hippolyte retreated. As the sun touched the hills' rim, one black walnut met the wild olive with too little force and flew out of Hippolyte's hand. "Your point," she said calmly. "Let's go for the daggers."

The cheering Greeks closed around Heracles, the Amazons around Hippolyte. When the circle reformed, Hippolyte grasped an ivory snake with an egg in its mouth, haft of an ancient dagger. A boarskin crescent protected her breasts. Heracles' shield spread from chin to knees, its boss carved with twelve serpents' heads whose jaws clashed with every footfall. The duel began.

Hippolyte's feet were nimbler, Heracles' stride longer. On one agile thrust, Hippolyte lopped off seven serpents' heads. At Heracles' next advance, he cut both tips from her cresent shield. The sun's afterglow turned purple. Then Heracles' dagger was on the ground, Hippolyte was sheathing hers. "My point," she said. "On to the starting mark."

Heracles stood befuddled, certain his thrust had sent her blade flying, yet the dagger on the ground was his. "Remember the goal," he muttered as he followed her to the mark. "When we reach the shore, I'll grind her bones."

A circle of torches lit the marble wrestling floor that crowned the headland. The score, so far, was tied. Heracles' lance was sunk deep in the side of Mount Hyrcania; Hippolyte's had flown farther but glanced off a boulder and now lay at the bottom of a ravine. The scale had balanced itself when Hippolyte's swift feet brought her first to the riverbank. Now Amazon and Greek alike held their breath as the warriors stripped and oiled their bodies. Hippolyte, ungirded, stepped to the edge of the cliff and drew back her arm. The golden girdle, gift of the hundred-handed one, sailed through the night. Spread on the waveless water, it sank slowly, carrying with it the moon's rays, down to the harbor floor. "There lies the prize," she said to Heracles. "Whoever is pinned first will watch the other dive for it."

He crowed. "You are skillful, little lady, and nimble of foot. But wrestling is my meat. On your guard." The match began.

All the while, the Olympian gods had been watching the duels, pondering the odds. Poseidon, latter-day god of the sea, annoyed that his darling had not long since clubbed the brazen Amazon to silence, tossed a giant crab into the ring. The razor pincer closed on Hippolyte's ankle. Heracles, chuckling, moved in to pin her—and found himself holding a small black mare whose sharp hoof shattered the crustaceous attacker. He blinked twice. When his eyes were wide again, his arm was pinned to his back and one knee was on the ground.

Then proud Athena, loyal to her father rather than to her gender, sent a stream of air to catch a torch's flame. Smoke filled Hippolyte's eyes. Heracles pressed his advantage to encircle her head with his arm and encircled instead a snake whose hiss pierced his bowels. He shook his head and found both knees pressed to the ground.

Zeus now wearied of the contest. "I did not beget a victorless warrior," he roared, "especially in a bout with a woman! Enough." His bellow became a whirlwind that spun Hippolyte around and lifted her into a cloud.

"Pinned by the elements!" Heracles shouted. "My whirlwind, my match!" He dove for the prize. The eager Greeks unsheathed their swords to begin their imagined final slaughter.

Underwater, Heracles found the goldspun belt guarded by a dog-like body topped by seven serpents' heads. He uprooted a submerged cypress and began clubbing. For every snake crushed, seven more appeared. He surfaced for air and found the headland dark, torches extinguished. Moonrays danced on a litter of broken swords. Panicked crewmen thrashed in the water. Beyond the harbor slip, two fireglows lit the night.

"Take your warrior gods' treachery back to the west!" Hippolyte stood on the headland, four black ravens restraining the whirlwind. "And take this message to your people: the Blackfog Sea belongs to free women."

"Vixen," yelled Heracles, "I will have at least your magic girdle." He dove again for the prize. Now forty-nine-headed, the hydra tattooed his arms, his thighs, his moon-shaped ass. A thousand fishes swarmed and carried him netted to the galley. He hauled himself over the rail, dragging the net behind him. As he stood shivering, the net caught the moon's rays and, one by one, the threads turned gold. Heracles narrowed his eyes. This could well be a warrior's belt, he thought. Who is to know it is fish-made?

In the sleeping quarters of the Great Hall, Hippolyte tucked a blanket over a child and blew out a candle. "You were right, sister," she whispered to Antiope. "They sail fierce ships, but their holds are filled with treachery. Still, no harm was done. Our warriors tested their mettle. If some Greek seed takes hold, we'll have newborns in our nurseries. We'll have to teach them manners, of course."

They slipped through starlit halls to their own narrow beds. The moon found its way to the western horizon. On the plain, a spindle-legged filly nuzzled its mother's flank. A cat in its mountain lair shifted sleeping haunches.

ANTIOPE

Themiscyra again
again the Blackfog Sea

The second Greek coming was different from the first.

The ram-snouted galleys made the same clean cut into the harbor and, as earlier, anchored just beyond the rocks that edged the shore. The crew furled sails and shipped oars with the same Greek flair. But where Heracles had been broad and bragging, this captain was lean, deferential.

He was a wayfarer, he said, a pilgrim in quest of knowledge. He had lived among the Cretans, had burnt sacrifice at the altar of their moon-goddess. He had heard in his travels of a city where you set your pace to the roar of a river. Beyond the city, he'd been told, the river watered a horse-filled plain and beyond the plain cascaded down a wall of sheer rock. Two days into the mountains, a boulder bigger than three ships guarded the river's source. It was a thing hurled from the sky, he'd been told, now half-buried in earth. Huge it was, and black and pitted. A thunderock, they called it, home to the goddess. He sought its wisdom.

His name was Theseus, and he offered as guest-gift a seal of the Cretan labyrinth.

Hippolyte was older now, her greeting wary: "Welcome to our city," as she handed him onto the shore. "You may set your pace to our river. At our hearthfire you'll find ears eager for your tales of Crete. But the thunderock, you must understand, is our sacred place; after this, we will not speak of it."

The fire ate hickory while Theseus painted the land of the Cretans. He drew Crane Dancers hobbling the slow love-dance, stepping onto a marble maze. He showed them bull leapers catching ribbons on the bulls' horns while somersaulting over their heads. He unraveled the magic ball of twine that had led him deep into the labyrinth, to the place of the bull-headed monster. The Amazons welcomed his tales and invited him to stay.

Antiope, drawn by this Greek's knowledge of the sea, stepped away from caution. Since their beginning, Amazons had lived at the water's edge, yet they shunned the sea, looking instead inland and traveling only by horse. When Theseus asked, "Why?" Antiope considered. Mama Thetis was of the sea. Amazons were of Mama Thetis. But no Amazon had ever held a steering oar nor felt a sail take up a gust and drive a keel through waves.

He told her about the winds. How a timid captain sets sail at the rising of the Pleiades and ships oars when they set, but he and others like him unfurl their sails at the first leafing of the fig and let the winds push them until the Bright Star of the North stands upright in the western sky. How the summer Etesians blow from west to east, but along the coast the land breezes of the day reverse the sea breezes of the evening, and flying gulls forecast the change. How, whatever the sail set, you always keep watch to the north, home of brutal Boreas whose blasts shred sails and drive ships onto rocks.

His voice was a zephyr, and his eyes reflected the sea. Antiope boarded his galley, determined to learn the way the same wind might sail a ship in two directions.

Sullen, Hippolyte watched from the cliff. At the evening hearthfire, she glared at her sister's rapt face. He will destroy us…, but she could not say it aloud. All ears were tuned to the bittersweet tale of the Cretan princess, his grief in losing her on a green island.

"He is not to be trusted." Away from the fire, in the room where they slept, she spewed her sister's speech from an earlier season. "Greeks are ruthless. They follow no laws of morality. He and his men will destroy us."

Antiope looked away, toward the stars. "See," she said, "they are the same luminous globes on land and on sea. We must learn seafaring, sister. The sea is our mother's home. Why isn't it ours?" The unanswerable question. "Remember, sister, the story of our coming to this shore. Our foremothers were abducted by sailors. The sailors slid into the sea. But the sails were set, and our foremothers lacked the skill to unset them. Some of our people still live on that far side of the sea. Without sails, we are cut off from them. This Greek can teach us the art of sailing. We might one day build a ship and travel to kin we've never known."

Hippolyte watched a star hurl itself into the sea. "And the thunderock? Will you take him into our sacred place?"

Antiope held her breath for a moment. "His question

is fair," she said. "If our mother is mother of all, why is her thunderock beyond the reach of a man?" She touched Hippolyte's arm and felt her shudder. "But I will respect our laws. His path will be only between his ship and our hearthfire."

Daily Hippolyte stood on the cliffs, watching the galley sail out on a morning breeze, sail in on an evening one. She was standing there when the messenger brought the news of the thunderock sundered, a chip smashed from the face. She turned only for a moment, to ask when? and lightning cracked behind her. She spun to an angry sea. Far out, no bigger than a gull, the ramsnout prow drove through a swell, forty oars lashing the waves, stern to the morning sun.

"Antiope!" she howled. The wind flung her speech into her mouth. She stared at the square stern of the galley until it disappeared into the morning mist.

Hippolyte and the warriors rode the rim of the Blackfog Sea, the sails of the Greeks always a shout beyond them. They hauled their horses onto rafts to ride the churning waters of the straits. From the farther shore, they descended into the land of the three-headed horsemen. The journey was long and dangerous. While they rode, the seasons turned. By the second leafing of the fig, Athens rose before them straddling a hill, facing the sea.

The Greeks were waiting for them. In a land where men let women pound laundry on river rocks or push beans into stony ground but never let them vault onto a mare's broad back to ride high, horsewomen rouse taletellers. News buzzed the countryside like black flies in a marsh. The Amazons found the Athenian plain smothered in chariots, men eager for blood.

As her sisters filled their quivers with arrows, Hippolyte cloaked herself in the dust of the battlefield and rode to the top of a hill that overlooked the Athenian palace. Had she been the sparrow hawk circling the royal courtyards, she might have seen three girls skipping, a boy drawing water from a well. She might have seen a woman pacing under a lemon tree, nursing a baby.

Hippolyte was no sparrow hawk nor could her mare sprout wings. She whistled and sent a shrill *"Antiope!"* across the brush-filled ravine that separated hill from palace. Above her, the hawk glided; below her, horses whinnied. Amazon blood, she thought, may soon seep into the plain. She whistled again and received an answering whistle, then another, closer. Antiope appeared from the ravine, Athens painted over her face, a baby on her hip. The women embraced.

What does a woman say to another come to rescue her from folly? How to explain letting caution dance on the waves, watching the wind instead of the shore? Or watching the changing wind, but missing the changing man? When he pinned her, her fury was no match for his muscle. After he showed her his trophy hacked from the thunderock, she knew she must walk Greek ways and watch for escape.

The boy was a yearling now, ready to be crowned with ivy and delivered to his father. The two women mounted the horse and rode past the astonished eyes of Greek captains and foot-soldiers. They found Theseus in his chariot, instructing the driver to seek the Amazon with the gold warrior's belt. Hippolyte took hold of the chariot's reins, Antiope thrust the baby forward. "The infant of the mother," she said, her voice a blade on a whetstone, "becomes the charge of the father."

Just as the mountain shadow grows with the afternoon sun, silence spread over the battlefield. The hawk of the hill caught an updraft and soared. Greek foot soldiers, charioteers, and captains watched their leader and waited.

"A battlefield is not a nursery!" His voice a wind from hell, his eyes no longer a reflection of the sea. "I tamed you, woman! Brought you from barbaria to civilization. You sleep on soft linen, your son is your honor. You are Queen of Athens. Go into the palace and see to your tasks. I am about to dispatch your sisters back to their animal savagery."

Murmurs among the soldiers. Hippolyte slid from her horse and stepped to the chariot.

"We do not provide queens for your bedroom nor raise boys for your army," she said. "Since Antiope is unarmed, I will challenge you, sword to sword. Should you defeat me, Antiope will return to the palace and raise your son. Otherwise, we Amazons, all of us, will leave you in peace."

Theseus jumped from his chariot and hefted his shield. "With your thunderock as my talisman," he shouted, "I have already won. Let us begin."

Sword suspended, Hippolyte stared at the black chip embedded in the center of the Greek shield, the gold jaws of a lion surrounding it. The thunderock shackled.

Hesitation, and the Greek sword swung. Blood blazed over her arm. She staggered under the blow, and Theseus swung again. "Athena," he called, "preside over my victory!"

Parthenogenetic Athena, who might have worn a goatskin pouch, who might have danced a gorgon dance, instead carried sword and shield. From Olympus, she saw her favorite Greek engaged in swordplay. She took the shape of a cock to fly toward the battlefield.

Picture it: The Amazons, arrows fitted to bows, grouped behind the two sisters. Flanking Theseus, Greek captains in chariots, spear-laden foot soldiers around them. Antiope and the baby on horse, the baby whimpering. Hippolyte has blocked a second blow, but one knee is on the ground, and Theseus looms, poised for a third, deadly, swing. High above them, the cock beats its downward path, but between cock and duelers, the sparrow hawk hovers, its wings beating, its rufous tail spread. An angry *kle-kle-kle* rasps the plain.

The scene rolls forward. The hawk dives between the blades. Its claws grip the gold lion; its beak dislodges the black chip. Theseus staggers back. The cock descends screeching, *Cak-cak-cak!* Claws dig into hawk flesh. Feathers and screams. Blood. Sacred stone in beak, the hawk tumbles into the dust. Hippolyte kneels over it, and stone replaces sword in the Amazon hand.

Athena, loyal to men, demands honor in them. In her presence, Theseus could not kill an unsworded challenger, especially a grieving one. Cock on shoulder, he waited. And as he waited, a damp sea fog thickened over the plain, obscuring horse from charioteer, spear from soldier. It lifted the dead hawk and carried it home to the hill. It lifted, too, the baby from Antiope's arms and floated him to the palace. It carried the Amazons—horses and arrows and all—across the Aegean and over the Blackfog Sea. The sun, returned to the Athenian plain, found Greek ears tuned to a bard singing an empty victory.

Arachne

Lydia
a spinning contest

Arachne spun by day and by night and with her threads wove sunset and dawn. Her loom was a story-telling loom. If a flying squirrel glided one night into the nest of another, by dawn its gliding was spread wide across the sky. If a snake slithered over a cypress knee and, meeting another, looped and entwined, sunset was streaked with twining and looping. Whatever the tale, the loom was the tattler. Nobody minded, the gossip was harmless. In those days, lust traveled in both directions. There wasn't a color for secrecy. Dawns were pink and mauve, sometimes streaked with grey; sunsets were red-rimmed orange.

But what if the snake were a goddess minding goddess business? Creating a shell, painting an egg, not eager to join with another? And what if some randy god knotted his snakeself around her?

Or, if the god were a quailcock pinning an unwilling quailhen? Or a rapacious boar covering a sow, her piglets scattered, squealing?

These happened, and more. Arachne's loom seethed. Blood-red smeared blue-black with fury and grief, dawn burned the eastern sky. Boats that embarked those mornings didn't come back to their moorings.

One morning Arachne sat next to a late-summer river. Her distaff held sumac and nightshade. A shadow darkened her spindle.

"Are you spinning my father again?" Athena, upright, owl-eyed, unsmiling, fingered a purple thread already warp on the loom. "He wasn't pleased with this morning's dawn, you know." She pulled the thread from its knot and rolled it between her fingers.

"And are you pleased with your father's engenderings?" Arachne kept her eyes on her own thread twisted between forefinger and thumb. Silence, except for the *burr-burr-burr* of the spindle. "He swallowed your mother whole, you know. She died slowly, smothered in his esophagus. Is that a pretty sunset? And you, you went from her belly to his head, but you didn't come out on your own. When the wedge split his skull, whose hand do you think guided the beetle?"

Athena turned abruptly. "Stories," she said. "Gossip. Anyone can tell tales." She smacked her sword against a rock. Two oak saplings shaped themselves into a loom. An elderberry became a spindle fat with threads. "We'll have a contest," she said. "The loom first filled will spread its story for sunset. Are you willing?"

"Is there a choice?"

As the relentless sun drove across the afternoon sky, the shuttles coursed: *thwap, churr, thwap, churr.* Nightshade and sumac grew across one loom, silver goathair and willow on the other. Strand after strand, the woof entered the warp. As the sun tipped toward the western horizon, Athena unknotted her loom and flung her cloth into the sky.

“There,” she said, ”is the true story. Victory to the father.”

Arachne watched the triumphant golds and silvers cloak the setting sun. She took her own cloth and floated it on the river. “Go,” she whispered. ”Sing high around one rock, sing low around another. Let the stories flow in many voices.”

Then she folded her loom into branches and multiplied her legs. She spins still. You can see her on an untraveled river path. Her web may shiver with white dawn. Or a struggling fly.

TROY

Fire forges strength. Troy burned, and those who survived the flames were tempered. Now they remember, and the torch they pass is fireground for the child.

An Amazon Beginning

a mountain in Thrace
years after the fall of Troy
a child and two old women

The old woman stared at the fire. I bit into an apple and waited. I knew there was more to her story, but the way she settled against the log told me that her tongue had gone to sleep. No more talk tonight, I grumbled. Mare's piss! Always scraps! I want the whole tale. I went out to tend the horses.

There were three of us on the mountain that winter—the old woman, Granny, and me. We'd all chosen a life away from the comings and goings of people: I'd run away from home, the old woman had found what she'd been searching for, and Granny? well, the cave was Granny's home.

The cave was more a rock house built into the side of the mountain that faced the rising sun. Inside, you could stand up straight only in the center, where the walls curved into a dome. Smoke from the fire spiraled through a hole at the top. We cooked and ate and slept in that room. Evenings, after dinner, we told stories. Mostly the old woman talked, but Granny had stories, too, and hers rode tunes. They'd start out of her mouth high, ringing against the walls; then they'd fall low and scurry like deermice. I wanted to sing stories, too. I reckoned that if I listened long enough and hard enough, my mouth would find the shape of them.

Singing isn't easy. You have to remember the names of the people and when they were born and where they traveled and who they met. At the same time, you have to fit the names and places to the ups and downs of the tune. I practiced singing to the horses when I fed them every night, but my songs were always full of holes—forgotten names, forgotten places. If I remembered the details, I often forgot the tune. That winter I listened hard because Granny sang less and I was afraid there'd come a time she'd stop forever.

We prayed in the cave, too, but not in the front room. At the back, in the shadows, a pair of rocks leaned against each other to make an arch. You ducked under and you were in the holy room. I wasn't allowed to go there alone, but as the moon waxed and waned, we went together to make the sacred bread. A fat clay oven squatted like a broody goose in the center of the room. I kindled pine branches and split oak logs to keep the blaze going. When it was steady, I took over the grinding from Granny. The old woman mixed the sacred flour, and Granny shaped it into round lumps. We chanted praisesongs while we worked. When the loaves were ready, we pushed the burning logs to the back of the oven and set the loaves at the edge of the fire.

On the other side of the oven was an altar where we put the baked loaves to cool. Next to the altar, a goddess sat on a throne. She scared me when I first saw her because she didn't look like the goddesses we had in the village. Her nose was a beak, her arms snaked around her broad belly, and her legs curved under wide hips.

Once, when I first came to the mountain, I had been kneeling at the grindstone too long. I got up suddenly and my head spun. I stumbled. I thought I was going to smash into the goddess, but she stopped me just before I fell. It was as if she'd strung the air around her with an invisible spider's web that caught me and held me swaying. Neither the old woman nor Granny said anything; they kept chanting, and when I'd caught my breath I went back to the grindstone and chanted, too.

In front of the cave, an elm stood guard, a tree Granny said was older than her great-great-grandmother, older than her great-great-grandmother's great-great-grandmother. When the limbs were bare, you could shinny up the trunk, step up branches like ladder rungs, and see the whole world below. A river flowed through the valley—a creek where it angled out of the forest but wider and wider as it slithered across the plain. Down in the valley I knew the river's loud song, but on the mountain it was silent as the hawks that glided from one jack pine to another.

I was born in the valley where the river runs. We had winter there, too, but the wind never screamed so hard nor stung my face with such cold. Spring came sooner down there. The river-ice could groan and crack and anemones poke through the snow; still, the mountain would be shrouded in grey. I know, because I waited every spring for Granny to visit. Only after the last of the fiddleheads had unfurled would her black mare appear on the ridge. She'd stay with us until her bundles of threads were sold and her saddlebags filled with barley and millet.

Evenings she'd sit at our fire and sing. My mother would be grinding barley, my sister stitching her dowry, and me, I'd be mending my father's good pants or one of my brother's shirts. Granny would twirl her spindle and fill the room with songs about strong women who rode fast horses out into the world. Antiope, Hippolyte, and Zerinthia rode flame-red mares to places called Smyrna and Sinope. They climbed mountains and passed through piney woods filled with talking hares. They yoked the east wind to build their cities and hung their secrets on a pair of laurels on a riverbank.

My mother didn't like the singing. Late at night I'd hear her complain to my father. "Women on horseback," she'd hiss, "acting as if they'd no hearth to tend."

My father would laugh and tell her the songs were harmless. "The days of the Amazons are over," he'd say. "Times have changed; let the children listen."

Once, when Granny and I were shelling peas in the yard, I asked her what made Amazons different from other women that they could ride in the world like men. She leaned close to me. "It's because we live without them," she whispered. Then she straightened her back. "Your mother doesn't understand. We don't shun men, you know. We barter with the iron-smelters for horseshoes; we trade skins for fish from the shore-dwellers. But the Gargarensians who father our children live in another place."

"How could they be fathers if they didn't live with you?" I remember asking, but Granny only stood up and rolled the peas into the pot of steaming barley. I looked toward my mother, pulling crusty loaves from the oven. She'd gotten my sister and me up before dawn to start the baking; we'd tended the cows and set the milk to clabber; we'd carried water from the spring and bundled clothes down to the flat river rocks to pound them clean. Now we were making the midday meal. My father and brothers would come in from the fields soon and they'd have worked hard, too. But when their bellies were full, they'd sleep while we spread the laundry on the quince tree and hung the dripping curds. In the evening they'd go off to the village plane tree and gossip with the other men while we bedded the animals and turned the cheese. If my father and brothers lived in another village, I thought, no one would sleep while someone else worked.

On the mountain that winter, it was just that way. Each of us had tasks: the old woman carded, Granny spun, I tended the horses; I fueled the fire, Granny ground barley, the old woman cooked. When we worked, we all worked; when we slept, we all slept. And around our evening fire, we shared stories.

The old woman's stories didn't ride tunes like Granny's, they fell out of her mouth in plain speech. She wasn't a born Amazon, either. She came from a place way to the south of our mountain, a place where the sun was warmer than ours and, even when it wasn't, rivers never turned to ice. She was born in a house that stood like a crane in the marsh, she said, but grew up in a marble-and-gold palace, slave to a princess. The city was called Troy, and it was built like a mountain with narrow streets at the bottom and bigger ones along the middle, and on the top, where the palace stood, wide courtyards with mulberry trees and finches. Every stone in the city wall was big as ten oxen, and the wooden gates that let you in and out were tall as the elm that guarded our mountain home.

I tried to imagine the view from the South Gate Tower. Only a thin green strip, she said, kept the blue Aegean from spilling into the harbor. Shadows on the horizon marked some island's mountains. To the south, the river Scamander foamed down from a green plateau and eddied through the lowlands. Behind the palace, a long finger of a ridge stretched toward the mountains. On top of the ridge—her eyes flashed when she said this—horses ran free. Merchants came from the farthest corners of the world to trade gold and jade for them.

Some nights the old woman had us jumping vine with her princess; others she carried us astride an old chestnut mare wandering the foothills of Mount Ida. Sometimes she filled the Trojan plain with bronze-wheeled chariots and men brandishing shields and swords. Her stories were as filled with wonder as Granny's songs, and, like the songs, came out of her mouth in pieces: the middle of one, the beginning of another. Once I asked her how they fit together. She said, "You're tall as a filly, but mares know where to crop." No answer at all, though it stopped my tongue.

On the longest night of the year, I was in the stable with my mare and Granny's black one and the old woman's piebald. The stable was a lean-to, its cracks daubed with mud, thatch for a roof. Next to it, a clay silo kept the barley mash dry. My mare was heavy with foal, and on that cold night, she was heaving. I was singing to her—one of Granny's stories, or at least as much of it as I remembered. I wanted to be awake when the little head poked out to sniff the world.

"Iphito!"

The old woman's voice cut through the night air, and I ran to the cave. Granny lay on her rugpile, her face a strange mask: one half calm as if she were sleeping, the other rigid and angry.

"Quick," the old woman whispered, "fan the fire! Set water to boil. And fetch me a hellebore—there's one blooming by the downpath. Dig around it so the roots come out whole."

I blew on the coals until the flames danced, then set the water jug over them. I knew exactly where the hellebore was. Carrying water past it every day, I wondered at its delicate winter-blooming flowers. By the time the tea was steeped, Granny's blue eyes were open, but her face was still a mask and her speech only gruntles. The old woman held her shoulders and dribbled tea into her mouth. I lit a lamp to Hecate and hung thyme over the bed to give her courage.

I left the old woman watching and ducked outside. It had started to snow, the first of the year. The flakes melted when they hit my cheeks and ran with my tears. "Hang on, Granny," I muttered, shivering, "I've got so much to learn." I begged Hecate for time, and she must have heard me; Granny's breath steadied through the night. Toward dawn I heard a groan from the stable and went out to tend the foaling mare.

The birth was a breech. The mare's coat was soaked, her eyes wild. A single tiny hoof hung under her tail. I'd seen lambs drop every spring and I knew the creatures came out headfirst and fast. I ran back to the cave.

"I'll tell you what to do, and you'll do it," the old

woman said. Her hands were comforting Granny who, like the mare, was soaked in sweat. "Likely one of the legs is twisted. Reach in your hand and turn it." I gulped. "You can do it," she said, "better than I—your hand won't tear her. Here, take this dittany." The handful of dry leaves she pulled out of her herb pouch filled the cave with the smell of mint. "Light these next to the mare's front feet. Stroke her nose to make her stand still. Then go round and do your job."

I did as she told me, and a colt slid into my waiting hands. I laid him on the straw, but he straightened his hind huckles. The front two followed, and he stood there wobbling. I turned to tend to the afterbirth and was astonished to see a second head poking its way into the cool dawn.

Stubborn mare. I might have known. The season other mares rutted, she'd frolicked away from the village stud. Then midwinter her berry had swelled, and she'd slipped the tether. I'd left the goats half-milked to search for her and found her at nightfall in the next valley romping on a mudbank with a grey stallion. My mother smacked me for acting like a boy, but my father said, "What do you expect? She's half-Amazon. Let her be." Then he said the foal, when it came, would be mine.

So that night I had twins. The colt, the difficult one, was grey like his daddy; the filly, who arrived in this world like water falling from a cleft, was flame-red with a white snip on her nose. Each foal found its way to a teat, and I left them nursing.

In the cave, Granny's jaw was still frozen, half mettled, half grooly. She was sitting up, though, and when I told her about the twins, she grunted through locked teeth. Suddenly one arm flailed, the other one still limp, and somehow I knew she wanted her stick. I let its silver horsehead catch her waving hand. She sat stiff on her rugpile, her useless legs sprawled, her eyes fixed on the fire. She sang. I stared at her. Unable to talk, she lifted her speech onto a tune and sent it soaring.

I sing of full-breasted Zerinthia
astride her black mare, a twin at each breast
she rides with the dawn…

Her voice stopped. Sweat beaded her brow, and the stick clattered to the floor. I turned to the old woman, astonished. "It happens that way sometimes," she said. "A song can live even when speech is gone." We turned Granny's body to rest. The song hung in the air, and I prayed to Hecate that it might be a horse to carry her into the spring.

The sun turned in its course, and the nights began to shorten. The northwind's rime stayed on the cave walls, though, no matter how much I stoked the fire. Granny learned to jam her distaff into her good arm's crook and twirl her spindlewhorl one-handed. I learned to understand her grunts and gurgles. Here and there speech tumbled out—upside-down, sideways, backward—and I'd listen hard to be able to repeat back to her what she was trying to say. When my guess was right, she'd clap her good hand against her thigh.

I told her about the filly stealing the colt's barley mash, and she told me about a horse who stole eggs from under a nesting hen. I said I'd seen lynx tracks in the snow, and she told me about a bobcat she'd killed as it stalked her mare and how she'd fed its orphaned litter until they were big enough to forage on their own. She cackled and whinnied; she growled and mewed. Still, while the wind howled, she grew bonier, and white wisps came out when I braided her hair. Some days she'd sleep all day; others she sat up but knocked her distaff aside, furious, and shook her good fist in the air. Sometimes her mutters turned to weeping, and the old woman would rock her until she slept again.

I'd hunted out the near woods, so I began to spend my mornings running the trapline on up the ridge as far as the divide. The snow was deep up there, and I strapped on rawhide webbing to keep from plunging waist-deep into a drift. I liked the silence in the woods—and then the sudden *dr-dr-dr-dr-dr* of a woodpecker grubbing its dinner. The tracks that crisscrossed each fresh fall of snow made me imagine a sleek shrew urging her family back to the burrow at dawn, a flying squirrel gliding out of a hollow tree to dance in the moonlight.

Sometimes, out in the still woods, I'd think about my family in the village and wonder if they missed me. I missed them. Even if the work wasn't fair, I missed the way my father swung me round when he came in from the fields and how my sister's baby lurched across the courtyard when they came to visit. I even missed my mother's rough hands sweeping my hair from my face to braid it.

The betrothal made me leave. The oaks had just begun to tip red when my mother told me to get ready to become a wife. I knew what marriage meant: go to a strange house and get scolded because you stir the soup the wrong way. My sister's husband's little brother hit her once because she told him to wipe up his own spilt milk, and then her husband didn't speak to her for days because she'd shamed him.

Kotys was the boy they'd chosen for me, and he didn't like the idea any better than I. He lived in the house where the path turns to the upper spring. I used to set down my water jug and walk with him halfway to the cow meadow. We weren't family, so we weren't supposed to talk, but I wanted to know about the world beyond our village, and he liked to speak his dreams.

The men under the plane tree had told him about a sea where rocks ride the waves and smash galleys, where sea monsters reach up from the depths to snatch cattle from the shore. Kotys said he'd welcome clashing rocks. He was going to take his father's piebald, he said, and find his way to the sea. He'd bend an oar on a merchant ship and sail to the uttermost bourne. I didn't tell him about my dream, about living in a world without men so everybody would work the same and no little boy could hit a grown woman.

After I heard about the betrothal, I decided to enter my dream. I waited for the late summer vintage. That was the best day of the year because we girls got to go out to pick grapes with the boys. Old Crimpfoot always wailed his reed pipe, and as the sun rolled westward, we'd smell lamb roasting all the way from the village square. After the hills had swallowed the sun, the boys would wind vines around themselves and try to make us think the vineyards were dancing.

I knew everyone would stay at the bonfire until the moon went to bed, so I slipped away and untied the full-bellied mare. My father had promised me her nestling, after all, so I thought I'd borrow her until she foaled and return her the following spring. I rode downstream, walked her across the ford, and started up the mountain.

LOVEPEARS

the mountain in Thrace
the old woman's coming

The leaves were crisp when the old woman came to the mountain. I'd been with Granny no more than a moonspan. I heard the shuffle-shuffle on the path and cocked my head. "Who...?" but before my question was out of my mouth, a wide body filled the whole cave entrance, and inside turned dark as night. A raw voice shouted as if Granny were on another mountain with a broad valley between: "Melanippe!"

Melanippe. I'd never heard Granny's name before. In the village, everyone called her Granny—my father, my mother, my sister, even Kotys who herded the cows in the meadow. Melanippe. *Black mare.* I looked at her sitting on her pile of rugs and heard her whisper, "Kin-kith!" I didn't know what kin-kith meant, but Granny looked like a parched grapevine drinking in a late-summer shower, and I knew the old woman was someone special.

The sun had dropped behind the ridge before the greetings were over. When the fire's hiss filled the space around us, I asked Granny where her name came from.

"It's an old Amazon name," she said, her ruckles moist with tears. "I was born with spindly legs and a headful of black hair. The midwife called me little foal, and my mother's sister named me Melanippe." She chuckled in the direction of her friend.

The old woman's several chins jiggled. "Sing her the namestory, Melanippe," she said softly. "Sing it the way you sang it to me."

Granny closed her eyes and gripped her cane. When the melody came out of her mouth, I recognized it. I'd heard her sing it in the village, but I hadn't known what it meant then.

Melanippe, daughter of Thetis,
Melanippe, born a black foal.

Granny stopped singing and rubbed her nose with her sleeve.

"Go on," said the old woman, "there's more to it than that."

Granny's face drooped. She let the cane fall from her hands and lay back on her rugs. "I don't remember," she muttered and closed her eyes.

I pulled the long-haired cloak over her and tucked it around her shoulders. "Sleep now." I wiped the wetness from her cheek. "I'll be host to your friend." I stroked her arm until I felt her breaths grow even. When I turned back to the fire, the old woman touched my shoulder.

"The first Amazon," she whispered. "She was named for the first Amazon. *That* Melanippe's mother is mother of us all."

We stared into the fire for a while, and then I asked her what her name was.

"Marpessa," she said and crossed her arms over the wide shelf of her breasts. "Marpessa, daughter of

Parthena and the spirit of the River Scamander." She snorted. "That's what they always said when some Trojan princeling had his way and left a slavewoman swelling: 'Oh, she bathed in the river, and her womb quickened.' My eleven brothers and sisters all had the same rivergod for a father, and we looked no more alike than kingfishers and sparrows."

"Marpessa." I rolled it over my tongue. I liked the sound of that name, too.

"That was my youngname," she continued. "When I was your age, my braids were red as the late summer creeper. Look at them now, white as dandelion puffs, and people call me old woman. 'Hey, old woman,' but I wear it like a crown. Old woman, wise blood. I'm travel-sore, child; I'll join Melanippe in sleep."

I had to get used to the way the old woman talked. One minute I'd be following her speech like tracks in a fresh snow, the next I'd be kneedeep in a drift wondering where the trail had gone. But she had stories, and I wanted to hear them. I learned patience.

Whenever the old woman told stories about the war, I had to work hard to keep in mind all the different people. Cassandra was easy to remember: she was the princess the old woman attended when they were both little girls, the one who told riddles nobody listened to. Priam was Cassandra's father, the king whose sister had been kept by the Greeks. Paris was Cassandra's brother who went to Greece to bring back his aunt and instead brought back....

"Tell me again who Paris brought back from Greece?" I asked one evening when our bowls of peas and barley were licked clean.

"Helen, moon-goddess of Sparta, sired by philandering Zeus and hatched from the egg of a swan." The old woman picked up her carder and began to work the wool on her lap.

"But she was married to the Spartan king."

"As was Paris to Oenone of the waterfall. It mattered little to either of them."

"But why did he want Helen?"

"She was beautiful. Aphrodite, some said, blinded him with love. Others of us thought he just wanted to see if he could entice her."

I hunched over, my head muddled. Even with the names in order, the war made no sense to me. Ten years of blood on the plain because a queen ran away with a prince? But the war was important. The old woman said it divided her life in two. Granny said it twisted her path. And Granny's mother, Penthesilea, died in it. The old woman had never finished *that* story. I chewed on the last heel of bread and decided I did not want to know about preening Paris or the Greek ships in the harbor or even about Cassandra and her prophecies. I wanted to hear the story of Penthesilea; I wanted to know the Amazon archer.

I gathered up the bowls and set them on the shelf over the grain jars. Then I turned to the fire and faced the old woman. "I am Iphito," I said, my voice ringing off the cave walls, "great-granddaughter of Penthesilea, warrior Amazon. Let me ride with *her* in battle. Let me know my warrior kin."

The old woman looked up at me and laughed. Granny grunted. "Sit, child-who-knows-so-well-what-she-wants-to-hear," the old woman said, "sit and listen. I'll tell you how my eyes saw her first."

the Amazon city of Themiscyra
the height of the Trojan War
the messenger from Troy

Penthesilea, warrior of the Amazons, leaned toward the red-braided stranger. Her body fit the burls of the oak throne as if the woman had grown from an acorn. Sunlight angling through the west window framed a slanting square on the mosaic floor. Outside, a child's chant wove itself around the *da-dum da-dum* of a two-footed gallop. Marpessa, eager to tell her tale, felt her tongue grow thick. She studied the sun-burnished patch of reds and yellows at her feet.

"Tell her," urged Melanippe, skinny as the stranger was round. "Tell her what you told me. Don't be shy." Melanippe turned to her mother. "Mama, she's a Trojan and she rode all the way from the Scamander plain. She brings news of the war and she carries a message to you from King Priam." She turned back to Marpessa. "Go on. Don't be afraid."

Penthesilea folded her hands and waited. Marpessa tried to corral the words that stampeded through her head but couldn't catch a single one to make a beginning.

"She's tired, Melanippe," said Penthesilea. "Take her to the river to wash the journey from her body. I'll call the council. We'll take the evening meal together in the dining hall. After she has eased her hunger and slaked her thirst, her tongue will be ready to story us." She smiled at Marpessa. "You've traveled well, my child. Choose your own time to speak."

Marpessa's eyes rose slowly from the floor. "Th-thank

you, Your Majesty," she stammered, hating the creeping flush that turned her cheeks red as her braids.

"Sst! No 'Your Majesty' here, child. I am Penthesilea, daughter of Cleite, no more, no less. Now go and let my daughter be a host to you."

Torches danced shadows over the ceiling as the river-bathed Marpessa followed Melanippe into the dining hall. A spitted deer's carcass made the firepit sing. Melanippe's knife sliced a chunk onto the plane leaf in Marpessa's hands. Their smiles met, and a flame fingered the coals.

Thirteen women—some wrinkled, some nursing babies, some no older than Marpessa herself—waited for them around the fire. Penthesilea held out a bronze cup. "Welcome to our hearth, young rider. Let your name enter the circle so that we may know you while we eat."

Marpessa settled herself on a rug woven red and black. She shifted the venison to one hand and took the offered wine. Her fingers read a raised acorn design while her eyes met the eyes of Penthesilea. "I am Marpessa, daughter of Parthena...." She hesitated; in Troy she would have added, "and of the river-god Scamander." But in Themiscyra, Cassandra had told her, Amazons count only by the mother. And so would she; Scamander had no face known to her anyway. Daughter of Parthena, lineage enough.

"Welcome, Marpessa, daughter of Parthena," echoed around the circle. Then silence, broken only by sizzles from the roasting-pit. The coals burned, and the spitted carcass became gristle and bone. A half-dozen dogs slipped through the shadows to carry back to their corners shanks still full of marrow. The greyest of the councillors rose.

"I am Cleite, the elder. I welcome you again to our circle. If your mouth is ready to speak, our ears are ready to listen."

Marpessa looked around the circle of waiting faces. She shivered in spite of the warmth of the smoky hall. Melanippe's hand lightly touched her own, and she let her breath out. Her tongue was ready.

She told them about the first time the crier ran through the streets, and how the horses were herded into hidden corrals, and how the marsh people brought their families inside the gates. Greek lances had rattled against the walls until summer's end; then the ships had disappeared. The seasons turned; the ships came back. Nine years of raiding, a few days here, a month there. Then one day the Greek ships sailed into the harbor and grew roots. Trojan grain fields became camps for the Thracian allies; the tents of the Lydians covered the fig orchards.

"I carry into your midst," said Marpessa, "this letter from King Priam." She pulled a yellow scroll from her pouch and offered it to Penthesilea.

Penthesilea shifted on her rug. "We are all councillors here. Read it to us all."

Marpessa read. "'Greetings to yourself and to your country. Thus says Priam, king of Troy, to Penthesilea, queen of Themiscyra. The ships of the Greeks have done great damage to my country and to others. If we do not vanquish them here, they will extend their boundaries into your Blackfog Sea. You whose warriors are invincible, I beg you come and join our cause. If we succeed in sending them back to their homeland, I promise you all the gold you can carry and more.' That is King Priam's message."

Murmurs circled the fire.

"It is a war of plunder, not honor."

"Priam's foolish son broke the code of guest courtesy, stealing away with the queen of his host. We cannot defend that."

"If the Greeks come into our Blackfog Sea, we'll send them back as our foremothers sent their Heracles back."

The murmurs rose and fell. Penthesilea silenced them with a wave of her hand. "Why does Priam think gold will persuade us to join cause in an honorless war?"

Marpessa set herself to deliver the second message, this from Cassandra who had foreseen the first response. But how to tell what she herself did not understand? She felt Melanippe's touch again and straightened her shoulders. "Cassandra, daughter of Priam and priestess of Apollo, speaks in riddles, but her thoughts are often beacons into the future. I will speak her words to you; make sense as you can." She closed her eyes to bring the image of Cassandra into her mind. Her mouth fell open, and Cassandra spoke with her tongue.

"The god-wrought sword of Achilles will pierce our Hector's heart. The arrows of Heracles will poison preening Paris with the blood of Medusa. A full-bellied horse will carry fire into the city. We are lost...unless the thunderock returns to its sacred home."

Marpessa opened her eyes and looked at Cleite, hoping for wisdom, but only the fire spoke. She sighed and continued in her own voice. "Achilles sulks in his tent for some slight offered him by the Greek commander. He's not shown his armor in battle for months nor let his warriors so much as sharpen a lance. Of the arrows of Heracles and the fire-bearing horse, I understand nothing." She paused.

"But the thunderock you know." Cleite's voice hissed with the fire.

A shiver ran through Marpessa's belly. She is like Cassandra, she thought, she sees things others do not. Aloud, "Yes, the thunderock I know. I felt its power in its sacred home on Ida. But Paris claimed the stone in Athena's name and set it in the citadel. Royal Trojans have no use for the mother—except to steal her power."

"Your Cassandra not only sees in a forward direction," said Cleite quietly, "she knows how to reach a distant people. She knows that when the mother's shrine is whole again, no fire will breach the city gates. She knows we Amazons may not care to protect stubborn men from falling into death's gaping maw, but our devotion to the mother binds us to carry the rock to its home."

Melanippe folded her hand over Marpessa's. Thoughtful faces stared into the fire.

Riding to Troy, the Amazon band followed an ancient trail that hugged the mountainsides and spanned chasms with long, swinging bridges. The moon grew round only twice, but two cycles was time enough for Marpessa to know she wanted to ride with Melanippe forever. She let her sure-footed dapple pick its way along the stony path while she marked the sun on Melanippe's black braids in front of her. When the trail broadened along a ridge, Marpessa let the dapple push forward until her knee brushed Melanippe's.

Melanippe laughed and held out her hand. "Are we kin-kith?" she asked.

Marpessa held her eyes steady on the dapple's mane, her hand holding the flesh that burned it. The path narrowed, and Melanippe's roan trotted ahead. That night, Marpessa tasted her first lovepear.

Lovepear? you ask. Where do you find a lovepear? Oh, you catch it with your eyes, let it slide down to your lips. It circles round your breasts and drops seeds into your heart.

And what does a lovepear look like? Oh, fuzzy like an early summer peach; or pale with petals that under your hungry tongue swell into a nubbled berry.

And how does a lovepear taste? Ah, the taste–like a hundred juicy seedpearls burst from a blush-red pomegranate, they fill your trembling mouth with briny nectar.

Daylight laughs: "Last one to the river is a nanny goat!" Or watches: "Steady, there, your dapple smells a bobcat." Or soothes: "Be brave, the thorn is deep." Starlight whispers: "There was a secret place on Ida where I rode…," and "Your hands are leather-strong, your touch is tender," and "I love the fit of us."

When the last of the mountains unrolled onto the Trojan plain, the dapple and the roan ran side by side, their riders free with the wind and rooted deep in love.

the mountain again
the firelight
the end, the beginning

I had said I wanted to hear about Penthesilea in battle, but when I heard the end of the tale, I wished my ears into blocks of wood. From lovepears in the mountains, the old woman took me to Troy where the Amazons marched through a city in shock. The Trojan Prince Hector was dead, King Priam lost in grief. When preening Paris failed to stop the Amazons from carrying away his sacred plunder, he schemed treachery. By the time the thunderock had found its mountain home again, Penthesilea had embraced dry earth.

"I saw her fall, child," the old woman said. "One moment she was high on her flame-red mare, her adamantine helmet glowing with the late sun's rays, her dagger parried. Then she was on the ground, vile Achilles over her. A dustcloud swallowed them. Athena's jealous anger, some said, that Amazons looked not to her but to the many-breasted mother. Others called it an evil deed of Zeus, he sworn not to lift a finger but still affronted by the thought of a warrior woman besting his darling Achilles. Wherever the dustcloud came from, it blinded her just the instant his spear thrust home. She was gone."

Tears wet the old woman's cheeks; Granny's eyes were running, too. I waited, afraid to break the silence with so much as a blink of my eye. I watched Granny reach out and touch the old woman's hand. Granny-Melanippe, old woman-Marpessa: lovers rooted deep.

I went out to look at the night sky. The Pleiades on the western horizon were saying goodbye to the stars of winter; to the east, the circle of Ariadne's crown forecast summer. I walked to the stable and kissed the filly's velvet nose, pulled a briar from the colt's fetlock. The mare nickered. Watching my equine family, I wondered about lovepears. I knew that love had to do with mating; the songs we sang at village weddings said so. And I knew about mating; I had watched animals since I could walk—rams with ewes, billy goats with nannies. When my sister and her husband came to visit, I sometimes lay awake while they rustled and groaned in their corner of the sleeping loft.

But mating didn't seem to me like lovepears. When the old woman told of the journey to Troy, the wrinkles on her face melted together, and Granny's mouth curled upward listening. They seemed then like those geese who shunned the ganders, nuzzled only each other's feathers, and spring after spring homed together to the meadow pond.

I walked toward the cave. The Pleiades had gone to bed and so should I, yet I lingered under the elm. I heard a groan from inside and turned to go and help. Then another groan, higher pitched, and another. I stopped. I understood that Granny was not in pain. The trail from Themiscyra to Troy saw only wild goats now, but Melanippe and Marpessa were tasting lovepears again.

THUNDEROCK

the mountain in Thrace
under the elm
under the stars

Great bear, baby bear, white swan, flying horse,
Little dolphin, water bearer, sea goat, fish!

I was practising the rhythm of the stars, marking their zigzag north to south the way Granny had taught me. Granny and I—this was before the old woman came to the mountain—were waiting for moonrise. We were ready for the bite of hoarfrost, but the night had brought summer to tease us. The leaves were on the ground except for a few stubborn oak clusters; the redstarts had turned into robins. But there we were, Granny and me, sitting barearmed under the elm. Thousands of fires lit up the night, and I was training my eyes to see them as flocks, each with its own name. Sometimes I pretended I was the chief shepherd, burning steady like the star that tells north, counting.

"A shooting star!" The white streak cut the sky and disappeared.

"Thunderock," said Granny, almost under her breath.

"Thunderock?" I waited. Granny didn't talk much. Sometimes I'd ask a question in the morning, and she'd answer me at dinner. Or she'd sing a song, and days later I'd realize she was telling me what I wanted to know. I looked back to the stars. Flying horse was upside down, so I twisted my head until it was right, riding toward the rising moon. By solstice, I knew, its nose would dip behind the ragged hills, but we'd see its long tail until spring.

"Another one!" I clapped my hands. "A thunderock! Two of them!" I decided to call it what she called it even if she wouldn't tell me why.

Granny cleared her throat. "A thunderock." Her voice was a rasp, and her breath came hard after it. She'd taken cold in the late summer rains, and sometimes she couldn't talk for all her coughing. "A thing hurled from the sky. It comes to earth to remind us."

"Remind us of what?" I asked, although I was pretty sure I knew. Even before I came to live on the mountain, Granny had instructed me in things of the goddess. I hugged my knees and called up my sacred knowledge: inside each of us is a fire that comes from our own star; when we die it carries us back. It was too dark to see Granny's face, but I knew she was waiting for me to answer my own question. "A thunderock tells us about the night-winged goddess," I said, my voice solemn, "she who kindles the starry fires and scatters them from her breast."

"Not tells us," corrected Granny. "A thunderock carries the goddess inside."

I tried to imagine a star carrying the goddess all the way to earth. Would the thunderock be a white fire? Would it burn everything it touched? What color would the goddess be? "Have you ever seen a thunderock up close?" I asked.

Silence stretched through the night.

"On the side of our mountain," she answered finally. "Among the oaks. Big. Black and shiny. Pockety holes all over it. We climbed there every year. Each of us tucked something into a pocket. River pebbles. A hawk's wish-bone." Granny gulped for air, then went on. "Wishes. They were wishes. First in a hoop race. A lost ring found." She coughed. "A baby sister."

"Baby sister?" Granny's talk always carried more questions than answers. I couldn't even think how to ask the next one, so I just echoed her and hoped she'd keep talking. She didn't, but before the moon had lifted itself off the horizon, she began to tap her canehead on the ground, a sure sign that a song was coming. It rose out of her scratchy throat, and I listened for my answer.

I sing of the eighth year, the great year
when snowdrifts cover the mountain.
We dance for the baby-wanting sisters
who climb to the crown and widen their sheaths
and carry home seeds in their bellies.

The song exploded into a thousand coughs, and I thudded Granny's back with the heel of my hand. She leaned against the elm. I started naming the starflocks again. "Great bear, baby bear, white swan, flying horse...," their names danced over my tongue until the full moon made them cover their faces. I watched for another thunderock, but the goddess had traveled enough for one night.

By the next full moon, the old woman had joined us on the mountain, and I found out that the thunderock wasn't only for Amazons. The Trojans had one, too, and the war turned around it.

Troy
years before the war
a slave and a princess

Outside walled Troy, where a river eddied down to a broad bay, huts poised like cranes in the reeds. In summer, the stilts rose from sun-baked mud and pools of water. In the winter, the river overflowed its banks, and water lapped the doorsteps.

Three paths led out of the marsh. The first followed the shore to the fig orchards. The second zigzagged through the fields next to a flat-topped ridge studded with pine trees and horses. The third became a road that led to the palace. Every dawn human bodies swarmed the bottomland–men and women and children resigned to another day of labor. Some took the wide road to the city gates, to potters' stalls, loom rooms, smithies and marble-cutteries. Others scrambled up the terraced banks to the fig orchards and the vineyards. Luckier ones, thought Marpessa, climbed the ridge to train horses.

Marpessa was born in a hut. The morning she first wailed, the queen gave birth to Cassandra. A herald called for a wet nurse and claimed her mother's full breasts for the palace. Mother and newborn were carried into the city where Cassandra suckled one nipple and Marpessa the other. Marpessa didn't see the reed hut or the brothers and sisters who lived there until Cassandra learned to drink milk from a gold cup. When she finally met them, they hung their heads at her linen dress and whispered behind their hands.

She grew away from toddlerhood and saw her marsh family only for the midwinter festival. Each year thirteen girls led the procession and danced the thunderock dance, but Marpessa was never chosen. "We learned the dances before," they told her. "There isn't time to teach you." She walked with her mother, lifting her feet to follow the steps and seizing the sounds of the praisesong. Each year she prayed for the sight of the thunderock, but each year, when the procession reached the foothills of Mount Ida, her mother drew her aside. "Cassandra is waiting," she would whisper, and Marpessa would bite her lips and turn away.

Marpessa's brother Jason was one of the lucky ones who climbed daily to the horses' ridge. Once she came to visit at midsummer, and he took her with him. Perched on the broad branch of a planetree, she watched him ride a chestnut mare into the herd and edge a dapple into a corral made out of pine saplings pushed into the ground. The dapple snorted and rolled its eyes, but Jason snapped a willow switch whenever it broke its trot. In the afternoon, Marpessa sat in front of her brother while he goaded a three-year-old into a prance. She flinched when the switch flicked the fetlocks. "They have to learn to step high," he told her. "The king doesn't like plodders." At dusk, he set her alone on the chestnut mare. Marpessa grasped the reins and slipped in the saddle until he told her to loosen her hands and grip with her knees. Twice to the pine grove and back, and she felt she was part of the mare. By the time she patted her new friend goodbye, the crescent moon lay on its back high over the city. From the foot of the ridge, she heard the chestnut nicker. "I want to train horses," she said, startled as Jason by the fire in her voice. He took her hand, and they trudged back to the marsh.

Cassandra, on her eighth festival of Apollo, was given a wooden stick-horse painted bright blue with silk tassels down its neck. She told her father that she needed another one for Marpessa. The king laughed and reminded her that a servant's place was to walk beside her and make sure no insect pierced royalty. Cassandra climbed into his lap and pulled both his ears. "Marpessa's my friend," she pouted. "I don't care if she's a slave." The king did not resist her charm, and the next day a second stick-horse—red with no silk tassels—appeared in the nursery. After that, the two girls romped their steeds every day—down from the palace to the broad terrace where the merchants lived, and on down to the lowest level with its hammering smiths and crying vendors.

Still, a stick-horse has neither a soft velvet nose nor recognition's nicker. Time and again Marpessa slipped away from her duties to climb the ridge and steal a ride on real flesh-and-blood. Cassandra scolded her; her mother beat her; once she was even brought before the queen. Marpessa nursed her pride and waited her chance to flee again.

One morning she headed the chestnut mare into the foothills of Mount Ida. Cassandra was in Apollo's temple preparing for priestly duties, and Marpessa knew no one would miss her till evening. She slipped out a side gate of the city, crossed a dry gully and climbed to the horses' ridge. Knowing Jason's thunder, she kept the main herd between her and the training ring. Finally astride the chestnut, she rode down onto the lower plain. The river eddied around rocks and under bare roots that curled off the bank. Hawks wheeled in the updraft, and the fields were blue with aster. Marpessa picked bearberries, savoring both the bittersweet juice of the fruit and the evergreen smell of the bush. She gave the mare her head, and they wandered into the foothills.

In a thick pine forest, the trail forked at a stone that stood upright and worn. Marpessa's hand was drawn to touch it as she passed, and a spark grazed her finger. She took the left fork, and the forest grew darker. No birdcall broke the stillness. Marpessa slipped off the mare and crept over the pine needles. When the trail spilled into a clearing, she squinted in the sudden sunlight. Through tears she saw the marble platform, round like a threshing floor, the black boulder filling a crater in front of it.

Marpessa, never permitted to dance for the goddess, had found the thunderock. It reached out to her. She knelt and embraced it and let warm currents flow through her.

Cassandra's thirteenth festival of Apollo was the dawn of her priestesshood. In the temple she would own nothing but her pledge, so the night before she left the palace, a giveaway was held. The queen and Cassandra's eleven sisters sat in a circle in the nursery, the littlest one a baby on her nursemaid's lap, the oldest nestling a child of her own. Marpessa and the other slaves-in-waiting hovered near the door, watching for a signal to whisk away a silver tray of oyster shells and replace it with a platter of roasted pheasant. Gold earrings, purple-veiled diadems, and jade pins left the heap in front of Cassandra, along with jars of must and myrrh, little clay monkeys, and a wooden stick-horse freshly painted and wearing new silk tassels.

"There," announced Cassandra when the floor in front of her was only polished tile, "I have no more to give. Enjoy my things with good health. I am ready to be priestess to Apollo."

The littlest sister threw her tortoise-shell rattle onto the floor. Marpessa scurried to fetch it. The queen lifted her hand.

"One more possession is yours to give," she said. "You must choose the one whom Marpessa will now serve. You may not have her with you in the temple."

Cassandra bit her lip. She was too old to pout and say, "Marpessa is my friend," and the king wasn't there to be charmed to her wish. She looked at Marpessa whose hands danced the tortoise shell around the fretting baby.

"Can I give her to anyone?" Cassandra asked. "Does it have to be a sister?"

"Anyone," answered the queen. "Or a place, if you like. The kitchen needs another cutter. You can give her to a person or a dutyplace, whatever you choose."

The baby threw the rattle again, again Marpessa retrieved it. Red shame crept up her neck. Whispers washed around the circle.

"Well, then," said Cassandra, "I give Marpessa—" Marpessa held the rattle rigid; the baby gurgled and batted it out of her hand "—I give Marpessa to Marpessa!"

Whispers burst into exclamations; Marpessa hurried after the rattle.

"It can't be done!" the queen exclaimed. "It isn't—you can't give a slave to a slave."

Cassandra met her mother's eye. "If I can give her to anyone," she said firmly, "then she is the anyone I give her to." She stood up. "Marpessa!" she called over the hubbub, "come into the circle. I have a gift for you." Marpessa, tortoise shell still in hand, edged stiffly between two sisters, who drew back to let her pass. The baby reached for the disappearing rattle and sent a long wail after it. "Marpessa," Cassandra said solemnly, pulling a ribbon from her braid, "I give you this blue band to wear in your hair. You belong to yourself now."

Cassandra threaded the ribbon into Marpessa's red braid. The baby screamed. Older sisters surrounded the queen while three younger ones began to organize a swap. Cassandra led Marpessa out of the nursery.

"You can go to your horses now," she whispered and kissed her on the cheek. "Come and see me when you can. They let visitors in the temple every new moon." She turned back toward the clamor. Marpessa touched the ribbon in her braid. One last look at the bright blue nursery door and she skipped down the hall.

On the horses' ridge the next morning, Jason frowned at her. "Girls can't be hostlers," he said. "They might have a position for you down in the fig orchard. I've got a friend...." Marpessa jerked the knife from his belt and sawed until her red braids lay on the ground between them. Her brother shrugged. "Of course," he said, "a boy who rides well is always welcome. I'll get you a tunic and boots. Smear some dust on your cheeks and make sure your chest is covered." Marpessa bent down and picked the blue ribbon out of the fallen braids. She tied it around her wrist and hurried after her brother.

She'd been in the yearling corral only three seasons when she saw the men with axes. Twenty or more of them snaked a line up the mountain. At the head of the line, a prancing white stallion carried Cassandra's brother, the one who came down from the mountain, the one who sailed to Greece, who brought back a foreign queen as his consort. Paris shouted directions from his perch. Before another season had turned, men drove a team of sixteen oxen up the wide, new road; at sundown that day, Marpessa and the other trainers watched astonished as men and oxen strained under the weight of a mountainous rock, black and shiny and pitted. The thunderock, torn from its sacred home, became Paris' tribute to Athena whose sword protected Troy from harm.

the mountain again
the goddess in another form

On clear nights that winter, I scanned the skies, hoping to catch another sight of the goddess, but all I saw was the flying horse inching upside-down toward the mountains. Most nights snow clouds screened the sky and blasts of wind kept my hood over my eyes. I worried about the foals, born too late to grow shaggy winter coats, but they kicked up their heels in the snow and chased one another. Sometimes they followed me when I checked my traps on the upper ridge. Where the snow was deep, they'd buckle their hocks and shoot themselves skyward, leaping over and over until I thought they'd drop.

The colt led me to the kingfisher. The filly had been bullying him as usual, butting his flank, then sprinting away. Miffed, he trotted across a frozen creek and up another slope. We had reached the end of the trapline, so I whistled after him. He whinnied. I started back down the trail, whistling over my shoulder. He nickered as if calling his sister to play, but she'd already disappeared into the pines ahead. I glanced back and saw him pawing the snow. He lowered his head and shook his mane—his usual invitation for a game of butt-me. Something was up there with him. I sighed and trudged across the creek. As I picked my way up the bank, I noticed a trail of delicate tracks with one birdfoot dug deeper than the other, the snow alongside mussed. When I reached the colt, I put my hand on his quivering flank and looked into the angry eye of a kingfisher. Perched lopsided on a fallen tree, one ruffled wing spread out on the snow, it shook its ragged crest and rattled at us. With a broken wing, I thought, how can it survive? I stepped gingerly past the colt. The kingfisher hopped once and then didn't resist me at all. I tucked it under my cape and, all the way home, felt its rapid heartbeat against my breast.

Granny helped me set the wing. The old woman said, "It's no use, she'll never fly again," but Granny grunted and spread her good hand to show me how to attach the splint. I settled the bird on the ledge over my rugpile and brought her some of the horse's barley meal.

"How do you know it's a she?" I asked the old woman as I watched the blue feathers nest into the straw I'd laid out.

"Look at her breast. Two bands across makes a lady." The old woman dipped into the pot on the fire and filled our three bowls with millet. "She doesn't belong here in the mountains, you know. She's a shore bird. In my country, her nesting time is now. The winds stop blowing, and the seas hush their waves. They say it's so she can build her nest on the flat calm of the water, but I've seen them setting eggs in the marsh."

Granny's good arm flailed, a sign for me to attend to her. Her hand skimmed a bird over the waves while her throat rattled the same song I'd heard on the trail. A sharp cry, and the hand-bird plunged, then rose struggling up past Granny's breast and over her head. It floated to a shoulder and hopped along an arm. Granny rattled again and looked hard at me.

"The kingfisher was injured down there and came up here to heal?" I watched her face to see how close my question was to her meaning.

Not close at all. I finally understood that Granny was

giving me goddess lessons again. Just as a thunderock carries the goddess down from the sky, a kingfisher carries her up into the mountains. No, that wasn't quite right. I closed my eyes and sat very still, the way Granny had taught me for thinking things out. As the thunderock hurls itself out of the sky, it changes from skywhite to earthblack. It's star and rock; it changes and it's the same. That was clear, but what about the kingfisher? She changed from a flying thing to a hopping thing, but she's still a kingfisher. I almost had it. I squeezed my eyes tighter. They popped open suddenly, almost as if they had their own figuring minds. I whispered into the fire, "Things change, but they're still the same." I didn't have to look to know that Granny's lopsided face was smiling.

I crawled to the ledge where the blue-feathered ball rested. I wanted to touch the kingfisher's crest, stroke her feathers, and tell her I'd care for her. I knew she was a wild thing, though, and my task ended with setting her wing and giving her somewhere to rest; her healing was her own. I could only watch and learn and someday, maybe, understand all the things my Granny knew but could no longer say.

Marks and Riddles

the mountain in Thrace
writing on the wall

"An eight-legged creature with two hands and two wings."

The three of us huddled around the fire, waiting for the spitted hare to turn crusty. The old woman and I were riddling each other; Granny was spinning her threads. The old woman had unknotted my riddle in a snake's blink, and I wanted to shake the tangles from hers just as fast. I looked to Granny for help. She whinnied softly. Ah, I thought, if I'm riding a horse, we're six-legged between us. Now how can I add two more legs? I looked at Granny again. She jerked her head at our splint-winged kingfisher pecking around the storage jars. I grinned. "It's me on the mare with the kingfisher on my head!" My turn again. "What goes over the water and under the water and still it never gets wet?"

The old woman frowned for only a minute. "An egg in a duck's belly." I sighed and turned the spit. The fire hissed at the drippings. "An egg," she repeated, "in a belly. My turn." She leaned forward and raked ashes from the edge of the fire. Her hand patted them smooth, and her finger drew marks in them. "Here," she said sitting back on her wide haunches, "is a riddle in a riddle." She hopped her finger along the marks and whispered, "A thousand Greek ships grew roots in the harbor, for every Greek ship, a thousand men fell."

I stared at the marks. I could feel Granny craning her neck to see, too. For a long moment the only sounds in the cave were the fire's hiss and the *t-t-t* of the kingfisher pecking.

"Give up?" The old woman chuckled her triumph. "Look. Here is a ship, and this mark makes it Greek. This one makes one ship a thousand." She pointed to the second group of marks. "Here's the harbor, and there are the roots."

"Is this another ship?" I pointed to a mark that looked like one of the first ones. She nodded. "And here's a thousand again!" After a poor start, I was doing fine.

"Yes. Now tell me what this is." The mark at the end of the row wasn't like any of the other marks. "Say the riddle," she suggested.

"A thousand Greek ships grew roots in our harbor," I muttered, "a thousand...men! That's a man." Of course it was a man; it even looked like a man with a sort of X for arms and legs and a round head on top. The marks were pictures after all! The shipmark looked like a ship and...oh, but the other marks didn't look much like what they meant. "How do you do it?" I asked.

"Answer the riddle, and I'll show you."

I'd forgotten it was a riddle. It didn't sound like a true riddle, more maybe something that really happened. I looked to Granny for help, but she was shaking her head at the fire. I was on my own. What was it the old woman had told me about Greek ships? I looked at the hare all brown and ready to eat. "War," I said softly. "It's the war you talk about. When the Greek ships came to Troy and everyone burned."

With her good arm, Granny jerked the harespit off its crutches and held it stiffly while the old woman pulled a leg into each of our bowls. It was as if a cloud had dropped over us, leaving us all in separate worlds. The riddling was over.

That night my dreams were full of dry bones, bones that came to life and danced stories. All through chores the next day, the strange marks scurried around my mind. I waited until nightfall; I waited until we'd all mopped the stewpot clean with our bread. When the fire was mostly coals, I raked a square of ashes. "I want to make marks that talk, too," I said to the old woman. "Show me."

She chuckled and put one finger into my ashes, plowed four splaying lines, and topped them with a dotted crescent. "Woman," she said. "You, me, Granny, whoever is female and has passed her first blood." I scrunched my eyes and saw in the splaying lines arms and legs, a head in the crescent. I trailed my finger over the marks. "Make one yourself," she said, and I wobbled my own set of furrows. One arm was too crooked, the other too straight. I plowed again and again until the woman at the end of the row was as good as the one at the start. I sat back to admire them, but the old woman's hand made them vanish like ducks in a morning mist.

"How many were there?"

I looked at the blank ashes. "Twelve?"

"Then draw just one woman and mark it a dozen." I frowned. "Go on, draw your woman." How did the lines go? I closed my eyes until I could see the pattern inside my head. There! Eyes open, I plowed my furrows, and planted a woman with her head held high. I grinned. The old woman's finger laid one line along the horizon, two pointing toward heaven. "Twelve women," she said.

I scratched my belly. What in the world...? Then I remembered the thousand ships. "Ten plus two," I shouted and clapped my hands. "What about a horse?" and a horse's head bloomed from the ash. I laughed at how easy it was. But then a goat was just two lines and a squiggle and a sheep the same except the squiggle turned the other way. I could almost see a loom in the marks for 'cloth,' and maybe the oil could have been a twisted olive tree, but in 'goatherd' I could see neither goat nor human. It wasn't simple at all.

I listened to the elm creaking outside. I knew flakes were flying. The old woman pulled a smoldering stick from the fire and spat on it. "Here," she said, "go bury it in the snow until its hiss is dead. A chunk of char is better than ash."

Charcoal in hand, I spent the rest of the evening covering the cave wall with pigs and cows, priestesses and kings, wine and wool and barley. The old woman directed my hand and told about the first time she'd seen marks.

Troy
before the war
skipping messages

Inside walled Troy, a woody vine slapped the cobbles with a steady skipping beat. Cassandra, just turned nine, lifted her embroidered hem, stepped into the upswing, and let the vine pass under her feet.

Forty-nine blackbirds singing on a wall

Two younger princesses tapped their toes, waiting, while Marpessa and another slave-companion turned the vine. A yellowthroat washed itself in a puddle caught in the dip of a paving stone.

Down came a bluejay, down came the wall

Cassandra stepped deliberately on the vine and held out her hand to Marpessa. "Find someone else to turn," she said to her sisters. "I have something to show Marpessa." The smaller of the two princesses wrinkled her nose and took the vine end. "Come," whispered Cassandra as she pulled Marpessa into the shadows, "there's no one there. We're going to the throne room."

Marpessa hung back. Clattering her stick horse in the marketplace, she was never shy satisfying her curiosity. "What are you making?" she'd ask a potter boldly—or demand of a baker, "May I have the one just out of the oven?" But the giant cypress door guarded a forbidden place. Slaves entered only through side doors.

Cassandra pushed the door until they could slip through the hall that stretched forever. Mosaics under their bare feet recorded centuries of kings and queens consorting with their heavenly counterparts. Cassandra danced Marpessa in and out of the marble columns. At the far end, a thread of sunshine captured dust motes over a chair covered with ivory and lapis. Marpessa held her breath.

"It's big enough for two," she whispered.

"Yes." Cassandra nodded. "When I was little, my mother sat there and talked as much as my father." She shrugged. "No more. My father says she upsets the councillors, and anyway, he says, this trouble with the Greeks is for men to decide."

"Who are the Greeks?" asked Marpessa, but, instead of answering, Cassandra pulled her behind the throne. A low door led into a dim and musty chamber. Rows of tiny holes looked like nests in a dovecote—except they weren't big enough for doves.

"Sparrows? Chickadees?" asked Marpessa.

Cassandra laughed. "Messages." She pulled out a scroll and waved it until it unfurled like a sail on an embarking ship. The sheet was wrinkled and covered with what looked to Marpessa like bird tracks in mud. "See this?" Cassandra ran her finger across the markings. "These signs carry another king's speech to my father." She lowered her voice. "Yesterday, the royal scribes drew a letter. My father's sister has stayed too long with the Greeks. The scribes scratched my father's sayings on the matter. Soon the king of Sparta will hear what my father says as if he himself were there." Marpessa had to lean forward to catch the hurried sounds. "It's a good thing he's not going, though, because they won't listen to him. There's going to be a *war*."

"War?" echoed Marpessa. "You mean like the boys play? With sticks and swords?"

"No." Cassandra's eyes seemed to be looking through

Marpessa. Her voice sounded as if it came from another room. "Real swords," she said, "blood." She held her hands out as if to ward off a blow. "A thousand Greek ships will grow roots in the harbor." Her voice was all chant. She closed her eyes. "For every Greek ship, a thousand will fall."

Marpessa shivered. The riddle had blown winter into the room. She tiptoed backward until she felt the mosaics under her feet, then turned and ran. Outside, the sun failed to smooth her goosebumps, and she didn't stop to catch her breath until she reached the skipping children.

Forty-nine blackbirds sitting on a wall.
Down came a bluejay to sing a new call,
down came a bluejay, down came the wall,
and the song of the blackbirds was over.

She tapped her foot in time until her heart found the steady beat.

"That rhyme's about my brothers."

Marpessa jumped. Cassandra had slipped up behind her. Marpessa set her jaw. It's just another riddle, she said to herself, and I can figure it out. Aloud, "You've got forty-nine brothers and...and...who's the bluejay?"

"My other brother. The one who lives on the mountain. The one nobody knows about. He'll be here soon. And the wall *will* come down." She stepped under the swinging vine. "Come–jump with me."

Cassandra skipped a hundred times without a miss. Marpessa clenched her teeth and forced her feet to clear the vine.

The mystery brother came down from the mountain the day of the royal games. There were chariot races and foot races, boxing matches and discus throws. All the men played in the royal games, but because the games were royal, the king's forty-nine sons always won.

The stranger first appeared in one of the boxing matches. He stunned the crowd by taking the crown. Then he toed to the mark for a footrace and captured another laurel wreath. The crowd buzzed. The princes' faces were grim with anger. The king chewed his lip. Cassandra dragged Marpessa to the royal bench. "He is our brother," she said to her father.

When Cassandra was small, she had been her father's favorite. Sometimes she sat on his lap in the council room and whispered in his ear and smiled when he repeated her whisperings to the councillors. After the day in the message room, she tried to tell him about Troy's danger. He laughed at her. When she tried to tell the councillors, he forbade her presence in the council room.

The day of the games, he frowned at her announcement. The princes were muttering; two had drawn their swords. The king didn't want bloodshed, but he didn't want a stranger breaking the rules. He waved her away. She ran like a hare to an old man at the edge of the field, snatched something from his hand, and ran back to the king.

"What your ears won't hear, your eyes must see!" she cried and danced a baby's bone rattle in front of him.

The queen jumped up; the king called, "Stay your swords!" Carved into the rattle was the royal insignia.

The king and queen gave Paris an ivy crown to wear to the victory banquet. The palace buzzed with the story of his birthcurse, the queen's dream of burning Troy. A seer had insisted the infant be killed, but the queen, a mother, gave the boy to a shepherd. He grew up on Mount Ida, tending flocks and taming bulls.

The princes welcomed their brother; the princesses fawned. A new moon came and went. The skipvine withered in the nursery. Cassandra stood apart from her sisters and watched her brother's charm work its way through the palace.

With all eyes on the new prince, Marpessa had no trouble slipping away to her horses. She wandered along the Scamander and into the foothills of Mount Ida. Some mornings she rode through meadows where high grasses tickled her toes; other days she let her mare pick a path through thick pines that closed off the light and then opened to let sunflecks fall onto moss cushions. She spent so much of that year wandering, she missed the gathering of the galleys, the oarsmen stepping into place, the ships, one by one, slipping out of the bay and onto the great sea. She came back one late afternoon to see a hundred sails billowing beyond the landspit, disappearing into the setting sun. Paris had sailed to Greece.

Cassandra withered like the skipvine. Her cheeks grew hollow, and her hair fell in tangles. She spent hours on the South Gate Tower watching the horizon where the ships had disappeared. Marpessa stayed with her sometimes but Cassandra almost never spoke, and when she did her words were senseless. "They're coming!" she cried one morning, her fingers digging into her cheeks. Marpessa looked and saw nothing. "There!" Cassandra repeated, "and there! and there!" With each "there" her body jerked until she was facing the Scamander. "Oh, Apollo," she whispered, "turn them back!"

Marpessa knew better than to ask her what she saw or who Apollo must turn back. She held her until the trembling stopped and then led her into the palace. The next day Cassandra left early for the temple, and Marpessa slipped away to the horses.

She found an Idan trail that climbed through a forest where acorns dropped *plunk!* onto the mare's flank. The forest floor muffled the hoofbeats, and whenever the wind blew Marpessa reached out both hands to catch a drifting leaf to tuck into her braids.

Her head was a crown of colors when she glimpsed the shadow moving behind the trees. Some shy animal, she thought, that kept pace with her, always just ahead, almost part of a tree or a bush or a fallen trunk. The path led to an oak guarding a wall of shiny black rock. Dappled water spilled into a pool. Marpessa slid off her mare and knelt to drink.

"Has he sailed?" The woman's reflection shattered into a thousand pieces as Marpessa raised her dripping face. The woman, an infant straddling her hip, bounced her mountain dialect around the rocks. "He has no business on the plain, king's son or no. He has flocks to tend and a child to father. Up here his self-love harms no one but a few bulls that he sets to goring one another. Down there he endangers a city, he threatens a people. If he sails, Troy burns."

Marpessa blinked and shook her head. This woman riddled like Cassandra. Marpessa pushed her shaking knees straight.

"W-who are you?" Black eyes flashed at her, and she looked down at the oak's roots.

"The new prince in the palace is the father of my son," the mountain voice shouted, "the man who carved my name into the bark of a hundred beeches. I am Oenone, and I was all he loved until conniving Aphrodite bribed him with promises. Is it too late? Has he sailed?"

Marpessa forced her eyes to meet the black ones. "The

fleet sailed on the new moon. The king wants his sister to come home. Paris went to fetch her."

Oenone lifted the infant over her head. "We are lost! He'll carry home a queen. A thousand Greek ships will besiege us. Troy will burn!"

A thousand Greek ships will grow roots in our harbor, echoed in Marpessa's ears. Oenone set the infant onto a mossy clump and knelt in front of the oak. She pulled a knife from her belt and chiseled a line that coiled back on itself like a snake. As she carved, her lips moved, and Marpessa caught fragments of a prayer that begged a goddess not to pour blood into the Scamander. The baby fretted; the snake grew. Marpessa stepped gingerly down the path, mare in tow. When the forest finally opened over the plain, she vaulted astride and gave the chestnut its head. The riddle was too confusing for a girl who had gone out only to feel the wind in her braids and watch the cranes fly south.

the mountain again
writing a song

I practised my marks all winter. The old woman showed me how some signs were sounds instead of things, but if you put them together, they could make a thing. Sometimes you drew one mark on top of another or inside it, other times you marched three or four in a row. You couldn't just do what you wanted, she said, and you couldn't make up your own marks. You had to do it the proper way or no one could speak what you drew.

Every morning I scratched signs on the ice covering the horses' water before I broke it. I drew a ship in the barley mash. I laid out straws just so on the stable floor and laughed when the filly ate up a king and a throne and a bronze chariot wheel. As I walked the trapline, I left rams and ewes along the trail so the wild ones could know they had kin in the villages. Sometimes the marks were still there when I came back; more often the wind blew snow from the trees to cover them, and I'd leave new ones for night creatures to guess.

One morning I ducked out of the cave and felt the mid-winter thaw. Long icicles fringed the lintel stone; the stream on the other side of the stable had broken through the crusted ice. I left my cape in the cave and welcomed the sun on my bare arms. I had to remind myself that the moon would swell three times more before the cranes flew north again.

After my chores, I half-slid along the trail below the cave. Down where the creek met wider water, dripping snow had softened the clay bank. I cut a chunk with my knife and brought it back to the elm in front of the cave. I picked out all the stones and smoothed the clay over a slab of pine. The clay was stubborn at first; my stick gouged the wood, slipped off the edge. Again and again I smoothed the surface. The old woman came out of the cave and watched over my shoulder. She didn't say anything, but I knew she liked my strong, steady marks.

"What shall I write? Why do people write?"

She settled herself on the flat stone bench and spread a bundle of sheep's wool onto her carder. "In Troy," she said as she combed the wool, "scribes wrote down the king's sayings so that he could speak to another king without setting foot in a ship." A redstart hopped onto a branch in the elm and fanned its orange tail. "When I lived with the Greeks, they made me write everything in the storeroom–jars of wheat, bundles of vetch, even the dippers of barley each of us was allotted for the winter."

"Why did they want you to write what was in the storeroom?"

"Just to know. Records, they called them." She wrestled a cockleburr from the wool and continued carding. "At harvest they wanted to know about every grain reaped to be sure no one held back more than was allowed. They wanted most of the crops for themselves."

"Who did?" I puzzled. "The farmers? But they grew the crops."

"No, no, the royal family. Even after the king was killed, they still had an army to feed. Every prince in the kingdom wanted the throne for himself. The army had to defend the lion gates from within as well as without. The farmers had to steal from their own fields to keep their babies alive. Some died anyway." The old woman snapped the carder and set her eyes on the flittering redstart.

I looked at my blank slab. I could write our stores, I

thought. I could write everything we have in our cave—barley and peas and wheat. But why? Even Granny with her dim eyes could count the stores; we knew what we had. A letter, then? Tell my mother and father about my life here on the mountain? But they knew no marks. We always shouted what we had to say.

I wandered out to the meadow where the colt and the filly were chasing each other. The kingfisher hopped after me, scolding. I lay down on a pile of dried twitch grass and watched three clouds skim the horizon. The sun pushed my eyelids together. I dreamed myself on a mare racing to catch up with Marpessa. She was riding into the morning sun, and all I could see were her braids and her horse's rump and tail. Then I was walking alone in a winter forest where beech trees with carved goddess eyes stared at me. A handful of shivering, dry leaves whispered in Granny's voice.

I woke to a grey sky. Winter had returned, but a fire burned inside me. The kingfisher must have seen my dream, because she left a blue wingfeather at my side. I set my tablet against my knees and began to push the quill while the flakes fell around me.

I sing of broad-boned Marpessa, her red braids crowned by sun.
She thunders into wild mountains, over windy peaks.
Her mare's hooves ring like cymbals....

Bloodshed

the mountain in Thrace
armor for listening

Spring came late that year, but when our guardian elm finally unfolded its leaves, Granny was still with us. Every morning I carried her outside and settled her where she could watch buds opening on the hobblebush. Our kingfisher wrestled worms from the loam by the stable where I planted peas and vetch. Her wing had mended, but she couldn't fly. She'd flutter lopsided to the mare's withers, pick a few lice and rattle a complaint. It hurt me that her wing wasn't right, but I had known when I set it that a broken wing can never be perfect again.

The old woman's firetalk that spring was about her days with the Amazons before they rode to join the Trojans in the war against the Greeks. Her speech blew away river mist and let me see the walls of Themiscyra high on the bluff over the Thermodon's tumbling waters.

The Thermodon, she said, begins in the mountain, where the water wells from under the Amazon thunderock. The water seeps until it can trickle, trickles until it flows, and leaves the mountain thundering. It courses the plain, carrying with it whatever stands in its way, its fickle banks leaving bare roots clawing air. Any spring morning, she said, you could hear an agony of creaking and a loud splash and know the river had collected another toll.

She made me see the well of rocks a stone's throw from the city, black rocks that swallowed the river and channeled it underground. I walked with her along the stone-paved streets, set my pace to the river. In the city's center, where three streets met under a vast plane tree, I watched the funnel of water spew up through a silver griffin and into a stone trough. I looked into the stables that sheltered the milchmares and nesting hens, the great hall where the councillors met and discussed their plans, the arsenal hung with bows of antelope horn. In fields east of the city, I watched young Amazons aim their arrows at apples tossed in the air while full warriors jumped horses over burning logs and drew bows at distant hares.

I wanted to be there myself, to test my own mettle. As I ran the trapline each morning, I searched out battlegear. The shield was easy. I took a half-dozen weathered hare-skins and cut them into the shape of a five-day moon. I layered the skins, one over another, until I could glance a stone off the shield with a high-pitched *thwang*. I stitched together two soft, cured skins, molded them around my head, and topped the helmet with a tail feather from the kingfisher. A flat rock curved on two ends and narrow in the middle made a double-headed axe.

The bow was the hardest. I was determined not to settle for one of whittled ash. I traveled five ridges before I found an antelope long dead from some cat's pawing, its skull twisted back over its ribcage. I scraped the ends of the horns until they fit together and greased them so they could flex. Once I'd woven a quiver out of vines and strung the bow with gut, I was ready to ride onto the Trojan plain to rescue the thunderock and send the Greeks back to the setting sun.

Evenings I whittled arrows, chipped stones into arrowheads, and filled my ears with the rhythm of the old woman's speech. I wanted to know more about the Amazon warriors in Troy. I knew my great-grandmother had died in that battle, but what about the other warriors? What about the thunderock? The old woman seemed in no hurry to leave Themiscyra, so I practiced patience. She'd tell it one day, and I'd be ready.

On afternoons when rain poured steadily, I scratched the whole battlefield onto the cavewall. I drew ships at the shoreline and named the Greeks: Agamemnon, the high prince who told the other Greeks what to do; Achilles, the warrior prince who wouldn't fight because he was mad at Agamemnon. Opposite the shoreline, I drew the walls of Troy and named the Trojans: Priam, the old king; Hector, the first son who commanded the troops; Paris, the pretty boy who courted Helen of Sparta and gave the Greeks excuse for the siege. I made a temple for Cassandra. Outside the city I drew Mount Ida for Oenone, Paris' deserted mountain wife. I drew a whole range of mountains for the Amazons: Penthesilea, first warrior, Granny's mother; Cleite the elder, Granny's granny; Melanippe, of course, Granny herself; and Marpessa who wasn't really an Amazon, but I wanted her there because she loved Melanippe.

The night the sun turned to travel again toward darkness, an old man who lived across the divide came to visit. He'd been on the mountain as long as Granny. He kept nannygoats for milk and always brought a little cheese with him when he came to visit. That night he brought a grouse, too. When the sun set, we pressed our foreheads against the elm and thanked the goddess for the longest day. I built a fire, and we ate grouse and early peas from my garden. Little by little the sky faded into night. When the claws of the scorpion brightened over the horizon, the old woman shifted, and I knew it was story time.

"You want to hear the whole of the battle on the Trojan plain," she said. "Tonight you'll hear it. Listen and remember: defeat is only the wind changing direction. The road we travel twists into sorrow sometimes, but pain is never useless."

Troy
the peak of the war
the Amazon encounter

"Hector is dead!" The Amazons rode into the city to find the marketplace humming with shock. "Hector is dead—who'll defend these gates now? We'll be throwing pots for the Greeks soon enough." Two worried merchants strapped leather coffers onto a donkey and muttered to each other, "Hector's dead, it's time to save what we can." In front of the palace, the Amazons found a cluster of royal women and attendants bloodying their cheeks with griefmarks and vying in a chorus of woe. Marpessa looked for Cassandra and found instead her own mother, Parthena, face drawn, eyes clear.

"Dismount, daughter, and hear the news." Marpessa slid off her mare and kissed her mother. The Amazons gathered around them. Parthena paused to welcome them, then faced Marpessa. "Just last week we watched our Hector lead the troops over the ramparts and into the Greek camp. We saw smoke billowing, and everyone ran to prepare the victory feast. Then the wind shifted." She pulled Marpessa along the street, beckoning the Amazons to follow. Standing on the South Gate Tower, she pointed to a lone chariot careening around the battlefield. Gaggles of Greeks cheered and threw lances into the air, but not a single Trojan soldier was in sight. "See how Achilles drags our Hector's body like a harrow behind his chariot? The barbarians have tormented us with this sight for three days now. Our army is paralyzed."

"Where is Cassandra?" Marpessa asked. "What does she say?"

"Shh!" Parthena leaned close and whispered. "Don't say her name aloud! She's locked away. Priam's orders. They argued. He said her gloom harmed our warriors. That was before Hector's death."

"You can take us to her?" asked Penthesilea.

"Not all of you. She's locked in the storage room. Let your warriors take their horses to the stable. You and Marpessa, follow me."

Except for a slight shaking of the reeds, the basket that imprisoned Cassandra could have been any storage basket. As they drew closer, they could hear her singing softly, "For every Greek ship, a thousand will fall...."

"Cassandra! We've come for you!" Marpessa whispered.

"A thousand men fall, Hector and all," flowed through the reeds.

Marpessa pulled at the leather straps holding the basket lid shut. "Cassandra! I'm back! With the Amazons. We've come to rescue the thunderock. We're going to Priam; if he doesn't listen to us, we'll go straight to the temple."

"Hector and Paris and Priam and all. We women will carry Greek babies."

The straps gave way to Penthesilea's knife, and the lifted lid revealed Cassandra's face streaked with mud, her eyes dead coals.

"It's one of her trances," said Marpessa. "Mother, can we hide her in the nursery? Can you take care of her?"

In the council hall, King Priam slumped, face in hands, shoulders quivering. His councillors quarrelled, each convinced that only his own plan would avert defeat. Marpessa and Melanippe lined up with the Amazon band on either side of the cypress doors.

Penthesilea pulled her feathered helmet from her head. "Greetings, Priam, king of Troy. As a falcon bears its crest, so may you bear your son's death. It's time for this bloodshed to end. Listen to our intent. While you go and ransom his body, we Amazons will restore the thunderock to its Idan sanctuary. The mother will be assuaged. The Greeks will accept the return of Helen and sail home. Peace will return to these walls."

Priam stared at her with glazed eyes. The councillors looked up from their mutterings. A bellow broke the astonished silence. Paris strode forward, his silver sword-belt clanking against a blue enamel breastplate. Under his helmet, his smooth pink cheeks puffed anger.

"The thunderock is mine! Helen is mine! The high command is mine! We will never negotiate. We'll drive them back to their ships. I myself will cut down the bastard Achilles." He turned to the councillors. "Who sent for these women? We have no need of women in this war, except to cheer our victories." He knelt and kissed Priam's hand. "Father, I have a plan. Listen! Achilles, I'm told, has eyes for my sister Polyxena. We'll offer her to him. She'll do what women do best to entice him into Apollo's temple. I'll hide behind the altar and, in his moment of weakness, I'll strike him down. Without his mad rampaging, we can drive the Greeks to their ships; then we'll set them ablaze. The war is almost over, Father. Give me your blessing."

The councillors jumped up, each clamoring for Priam's attention. Penthesilea motioned her warriors outside where Cassandra was waiting, her eyes burning fire again.

"My pretty brother is full of himself, and my father's confused. Let them argue; we can return the thunderock without their help." She gripped Marpessa's arm. "Show them to Athena's temple. The old man who sells firewood will lend you his ox and cart. Once we've lifted it onto the cart, you and a handful can manage alone. The sentry at the east gate will let you pass. Wait at the waterfall. I'll send a message to Oenone; she can guide you to the sacred grove." She turned to Penthesilea. "You and the rest of the warriors must stay here. Once the thunderock is safely home, Priam will negotiate. He'll need your warriors as go-betweens."

Inside the temple, the thunderock rested on a low pillar in front of Athena. A priestess stretched to pour oil into a hanging lamp. Cassandra touched her arm and whispered. The priestess shook her head, horror on her face. Another joined them, then another. Cassandra's whisper took body and shrilled, "It must be returned, else we perish in flames!"

A priest appeared, heavy brows squaring his face. "Go back to your own temple, go back to your weeping Apollo. We have no need of your gloom here. Take these heathen women from this sacred place."

Thirteen Amazons set themselves shoulder to shoulder, a wall of crescent shields between the servants of Athena and the sacred black stone. Another twelve knelt and began to maneuver it. The ox cart groaned as it rolled down the ramp. Shouts from the palace joined the uproar in the temple. Paris thundered over the clamor, "No! Athena will be angry! She is our protector!" In antiphony, Penthesilea cried, "Stand back! The stone is sacred to the mother! Your city will be a torch unless you give it up."

The Amazons waited six days at the waterfall, but Oenone did not come. Marpessa tried to call up the memory of that gone-by morning when her legs barely straddled the chestnut mare.

"I can see the path in my head," she whispered to Melanippe. "There were berry bushes first and then thick pines. An upright stone marked the fork. I can see it clearly."

Ida had changed, of course. Ten years of foraging Greeks had left slashes on its sides—whole stands of oak cut down to build ramparts, footpaths broadened to mud tracks for ox carts. Marpessa wept in frustration. "Oenone," she called into the trees, "where are you?"

A new direction on the seventh day led them past one of the secret corrals where healing Trojan horses awaited new battle duty. The gate was broken, the horses bloody carrion. Marpessa stared at the dead animals. "Why slaughter them?" rasped Melanippe. "Why not steal them? I don't understand these Greeks. They drag a corpse around the battlefield; they butcher sacred animals. Hide the thunderock at the waterfall, and we'll go back to Troy. If my mother is fighting, she'll need me by her side."

Marpessa turned dry eyes to her. "You go. I will keep searching. Hide the rock and take the warriors with you. I'll come get you when I've found the sacred crater." They held each other briefly, then Melanippe left running.

Days later, when Marpessa found the berry bushes, the thick pines, and the upright stone, the sacred grove looked like the secret corral. The stones of the dancing floor were scattered and broken, the circle of trees uprooted and burned. The crater that once held the sacred rock was an open grave for thirteen smashed skulls and a pile of bones picked clean by vultures. Tears that failed to come for dead horses fell now for sisters Marpessa had never known.

Melanippe found her in a rebuilt sanctuary, each broken stone of the dancing floor carefully fitted to its partner. The uprooted trees had been dragged clear; fresh-planted seedlings wavered in a circle. In front of the dancing platform, the thunderock rested in its crater, polished to a black shine. Marpessa sat next to it scratching moon signs into the dirt. "She's gone," she said without looking up. "There's no power in the rock. Touch it yourself and see. There's nothing there. She's gone."

Melanippe sank beside her. "They're all gone. Troy is burning."

On an outcropping that overlooked the city, Marpessa and Melanippe watched smoke belch from the towers. Toy soldiers darted along the walls flinging miniature chests and baby cribs down to the rocks below. Others herded stumbling dolls past the charred splinters of the South Gate. Between the burning city and the waiting Greek ships, the battlefield was littered with unwheeled chariots, dead horses still in traces. Beyond, the blood-red Scamander eddied around lifeless puppets whose battlegear, caught on rock or overhanging limb, held them from rushing seaward with the flood. Hawks wheeled over the city and whistled to one another, but neither the cries of the living nor the groans of the dying reached the ledge. The still air was broken only by the dull rapping of a woodpecker searching out grubs in a leafless tree.

"Oenone failed to meet us at the waterfall because she was with Paris." Melanippe's voice was edged with grief. "Your friend Cassandra told me. Paris was dying. Oenone took her herbs to cure him—too late. He died even as he drank her potion."

Marpessa shook her head. Oenone, Oenone, she cried to herself, How could you forsake the mother for a man who deserted you? "And how did Paris die?"

"Prancing on the city wall, bragging." Melanippe shrugged. "He had just killed Achilles. He wanted to taunt the Greeks. He held up Achilles' shield to let the Greeks know it no longer graced their hero. It weighed too much, and he stumbled. An arrow flew up from the plains and caught him under the breastbone. Cassandra called it an arrow of Heracles dipped in the blood of Medusa."

"And how did Paris kill Achilles? He wasn't his equal."

Silence. The woodpecker gave up its dead tree and flew to another.

"He caught him in the temple of Apollo. Do you remember his proposal in the council chamber? He did it. He bartered his sister for the battleplan of the Greeks. Achilles came unarmed. Paris hid with his short bow behind the altar. He shamed his sister, then sent his arrow home."

The woodpecker's rapping began again. The herd of dolls was halfway to the ships. The wind, shifting, brought the faint smell of burning wood, burning leather, burning flesh. Marpessa could not bear not knowing any longer.

"Penthesilea," she whispered, "your mother, where is she?" She felt Melanippe's fist clench at her side, her chest tighten. Then, like the sails of a ship that changes course and spills the wind, Melanippe's body slackened. Her voice took on the dead tone of a cracked flute.

"Killed by Achilles. Killed by the hand of Achilles through the tongue of Paris. Priam, he told her, had persuaded him to give up Helen. He would honor his father, Paris said. To witness the peacemaking, he needed a warrior unbound to either cause. She took him at his word and rode, armed only with her dirk, to the designated willow by the Scamander. As she rode, he plotted with Achilles the trade of his sister and told the brute that only the Amazon stood between him and his longed-for Polyxena."

Marpessa closed her eyes so that she could see neither the smoke of the city nor the band of Trojan women and children stepping up the Greek gangplanks into slavery. Enough, she thought. I don't want to hear how he stalked her waiting to talk peace, how he used the power of his lance against her short sword, how he unhorsed her and ended her life. Let that much be unknown to me. But the lidless eye of her mind watched, over and over, the fall of the Amazon warrior, the dying of Penthesilea.

"It's time now!" Melanippe's whisper shattered the falling shadow. "The sun's touched the sea. Cleite and I rescued her body. The dark will cover us while we send her on her journey to the other world."

Penthesilea rested on a bier of oak logs hidden in a gully in the foothills above the battlefield. Clouds covered the moon, but a single torch revealed her braids decked with wild celery, her feet covered with grapevines and myrtle. Cleite and a dozen Amazon warriors squatted around the bier, their voices filling the gully with a monotonous keen. Melanippe pulled out her knife, cut off her own braids, and laid them on the crescent shield that covered her mother's breast. Marpessa wove a tuft of marjoram into the celery crown. The sickle moon broke through the clouds for a moment and was swallowed again. The keening ended, Cleite handed the torch to Melanippe.

"Send it home!" she rasped. "Let her who once was fire become ash. Let ash renew the earth."

The pyre burned through the night. The wind that whipped sparks from the flames scattered the laments for the wandering soul. By the time the grey east had melted to red, the red coals had burned grey. Cleite quenched the last glow with river-water. They sifted the ashes until the white bones lay in a pile. Cleite placed them one by one into a leather pouch.

"Did you tell her how she fell?" Cleite put her hand on Melanippe's shoulder.

"I told her."

"All of it?"

"No."

"You must tell her. She has a right to know. She's one of us now. Amazons do not shun the truth, even when it's bitter."

Melanippe pulled away and walked to the center of the ashes. She stooped and rubbed her hands in ash, then streaked her face grey.

"All right, she will know." She climbed the gully's bank and stood next to a wind-bent hawthorn. Marpessa followed, not wanting to know, not wanting not to know. "This Achilles was a madman." Melanippe's voice was hard. "He killed her, yes, and could not stop killing. First his spear, then his sword, then, as the life flowed out of her, the blade between his legs. May his soul wander in the nether forever; may he thirst and find only piss; may his sons and his sons' sons die dishonored far from home."

Marpessa had eaten only berries and wild asparagus for days, yet her stomach threw up what it could. Her body, feeling too much pain, unleashed her, and she drifted away. What was left of her perched on the topmost branch of the hawthorn. She stared down past her own body and fixed her eye on a tuft of dry grass that one moment rippled with windstrokes and the next stood still. A dove beside her mourned, *Ooah, cooo, cooo, cooo.*

Sun spilling into the gully broke the spell. Marpessa regained her body and embraced Melanippe. "I share your grief, kin-kith. As a she-lion bears her young, so may we bear our pain."

Cleite waved. "Come," she called, "we'll carry her bones to Themiscyra. Amazons have died before, and Amazons will die again; the living go on living. You are one of us now; you will follow our ways."

the mountain again
the end of the story

The fire hissed. I had no heart to poke its embers into flames. I'd heard what I'd wanted to hear; I could not unhear it.

The old man stood. "War does that to men. We can't tell ourselves from our weapons. I was there at your battle of Troy. The Greeks were barbarians, the Trojans no better. I foraged your Mount Ida once with men crazed from seeing the guts of their comrades spilled day after day. We stumbled on a circle of dancing women and smashed their skulls for the joy of smashing. War was a whore, we said, and whores were women. I was ashamed; I ran away. I wandered until I became human again; this mountain holds me human." He saluted us and ducked out of the cave.

I kicked a log into the fire so hard sparks scattered onto the cave floor. I watched the red glow burst into flame and dance crazy shadows on the cave walls. My mind was full of horrors but, like a summer gnat, a question buzzed through my thoughts. "When you first came to this cave," I finally asked the old woman, "you told me you had seen with your own eyes how Penthesilea fell. Tonight you tell me you were with the thunderock on Mount Ida. How can both be true?"

The old woman walked to the doorway. I couldn't see the stars beyond her broad body, but I knew the four corners of Libra glowed dead ahead of her. "We see some things with our eyes as we watch them," she said, "and some things we see only inside our heads. Both sights are carved into us." She turned around and let the fireglow touch her face. "Can *you* see Penthesilea falling?" she asked, and I nodded. I rubbed the tears that wet my face but I knew no rubbing would erase the clay of my mind.

"You've forgotten what I told you." Her voice was almost hard. "There is no defeat. Ever. There's only a change of direction, only a new path to follow. Do you understand?" I nodded, although her meaning was nothing I could grasp.

Granny grunted. The old woman knelt beside her. I watched them touch hands. "Our paths forked that day." The old woman's voice was gentle again. "Carousing Greeks caught us as we skirted the battlefield searching for our homeward trail. We fought them, but one brute swung me like a lamb over his shoulder. He ran while the other men jabbed their swords. Down by the Scamander, he sold me to Agamemnon's helmsman, and I was herded into the stinking hold of a ship. I fought rats as big as my fists for a place to crouch, but I didn't give my voice to the moans around me. I was an Amazon and loved by an Amazon. When the creaking oars told us we were underway, I knew she was there on the shore. And she would follow me. I might be a slave for years, but she would find me."

The old woman shifted until she lay next to Granny, her arms cradling Granny's head. I looked from them to the fire. In the flames, I saw Greek ships slide out to sea, Melanippe on the deserted shore. And clear as the rattle of our kingfisher, I heard the call skip over the night waves: *I will find you, kin-kith, I will find you.*

Exile

Water sunders lands and families,
swelling her depth with tears of exile.

Migration

off the coast of Crete
just after the fall of Troy
an Amazon and a helmsman

The ship was a fifty-oared galley with a full-bellied sail. Oars shipped, the crew watched for signs of a changing wind. At the stern, the helmsman braced his bulk against the steering oar.

Marpessa stood on the small foredeck and eyed the progress of the twenty or more ships spread out behind them on the grey-green sea. A gust drove the gunwale almost into the water. She welcomed the spray in her face. The slavehold, where she'd been only moments before, was filthy with human misery. What is the price of this bracing freedom? she thought, and then pulled her attention to the soothing voice beside her.

"The wind's been against us since we left Troy," Cassandra was saying. "We had to skirt along the coast. Only this morning we made the turn toward Crete. But tonight you'll see how the Pleiades are already disappearing into the sea. We cannot reach Greece before the winter storms begin." A tremor moved across her face. "Agamemnon says there are Cretans who owe us. We'll be safe there." A short pause, then a whisper. "Safer there than in his homeland."

Marpessa stared at a flapping sail corner. "More burning cities?"

"No. His city won't burn. But ten years without a king...do you imagine everyone will celebrate his return?"

"Say what you mean."

"I dream. Every night since he forced me into his bed. Again and again I see wild dogs ravaging peacocks, scattering their feathers and bones. The biggest dog runs bloody-mouthed into the woods. When he reaches his lair, a cypress has fallen over it." She shook her head. "Agamemnon won't live to see his son become a man."

Marpessa stared out to sea. Too many shadows, she thought, she sees too many shadows. Always invisible to the rest of us and then suddenly they loom up and smother us. Enough. I don't want to hear about shadows.

She felt Cassandra's hand in her own hand, leading her away from the rail. "Come on," Cassandra said. "I'll take you to my cabin and smooth your back with oil."

Agamemnon's cabin glittered with spoils. Marpessa picked her way through piles of shields and greaves and bloody swords, all flaunting the victor's might. A girl she might once have known scurried away from a bronze tub in a corner. Rising steam welcomed her. She closed her eyes and let her mind empty until all she knew was water and oil, Cassandra's hands kneading her knotted back and Cassandra's voice remembering days in the nursery.

A bell clanged, and a pitcherful of cold water dowsed her awake. Before her mouth could form a protest, she was dressed: a long skirt swished from her waist, a silk blouse draped her breasts. Cassandra laid a finger across her lips.

"You've grown full and round since we bathed

ourselves in the nursery. You can't pass for a boy any more. Your limbs are tight with muscles, but you've got the belly and breasts of a woman. A Trojan woman, I'm afraid; Agamemnon won't let you be an Amazon. He wants you in women's clothes when you meet Thalas."

Marpessa's tongue fumbled. "Thalas?"

"Thalas, the helmsman. The man who bought you from that soldier. You belong to him now." She shook her head. "The world's upside-down, Marpessa. We have no wills of our own. Accept divine will. Your path will turn again another year."

"No," hissed Marpessa. "I'll go back to the hold, I'll...."

"Dearest, they know where you've been hiding. If you go back...." Her voice hung in the air.

Marpessa didn't need Cassandra's visions to tell her what she already knew. Nightly, when the ship anchored in some cove of some offshore island, the crew left their oars and scrambled into the hold. A contest, they called it, to prove their stamina. Nightly Marpessa had hidden herself between two horses, covering her ears against the whoops and the screams.

"It's not so bad up here," said Cassandra. "Alone, behind closed doors, they turn into little boys, you know. All that bellowing's for each other. In this chamber, Agamemnon's gentle as a pigeon. He wants his praise; he wants his brow stroked. Give him that, and he's happy as a suckling." She stroked Marpessa's cheek. "I'm sorry. I should have let you stay hidden. But there isn't any choice now."

A shadow fell across the cabin doorway. "Bath done?" It was almost a growl.

"Forgive me," Cassandra whispered and kissed Marpessa's forehead. When Marpessa looked up, she was alone in the cabin with the helmsman.

He was big as a mountain, tall as a cypress, but for all that flesh and bone, his head was small, perched like an eagle's nest on a boulder. Grey flecked his beard, and stringy hair roped over his ears like seaweed. He frowned down at Marpessa.

"I did that to a pretty woman?" He reached toward a bruise on her cheek. She flinched and backed against the cabin wall, her fist hidden in the fold of her skirt. His hand dropped to his side and flipped like a fish on a bank. "Well, um...." He stepped backward and shrugged. "I'm Thalas, helmsman. This ship is mine to guide. Umm..., you're Marpessa, they tell me." Marpessa stared at him. "I thought you were a boy, you know. That's why I bought you. When all these soldiers go back to their fields, I'll need a new crew. You looked strong and healthy, but when you struggled, I...." He twisted his lip. "Well, I'm sorry. You're a woman; I'll treat you well. Come on, I'll show you our quarters."

Marpessa unclenched her fist. The speech was gruff, but the eyes–black beads set narrow over weathered cheeks–were not evil. She followed him into the passageway and saw that, for all his bulk, he stepped lightly like a dancer. He led her into a cabin as sparsely furnished as Agamemnon's was cluttered with plunder.

"Well," he said, sweeping his arm around the room, "this is the nest." She eyed the single bunk. "Oh, don't worry. You can see it's only big enough for my frame. We'll lay a mat on the floor for you tonight. Tomorrow we'll sleep in Crete. I won't touch you by force. I know how you see us Greeks, but...uh...I don't...there are no rights of the victors in here. You're safer with me than in your horses' hold. Someone would have found you eventually."

He reached down a loaf of bread from a shelf and carved a hunk with his knife. Until that moment,

Marpessa had forgotten her hunger. Whatever might come, she wasn't going to be hurt right now. She chewed the bread slowly, rolling its barley taste over her tongue.

"There's cheese, too. A change from horses' mash, eh?"

She took the yellow chunk and bit into a field of Trojan clover. For the first time since she'd found the smashed sanctuary on the mountain, tears stung her eyes. Troy was gone. The princesses she'd grown up with were scattered onto these ships with her sisters from the marsh. Slaves, all slaves now. Her brothers, she supposed, were dead. Jason, the horsebreaker, had driven Hector's chariot and died with him. How the others had died, or whether they'd escaped into the mountains, she would never know. And so many foals she'd helped bring into this world, had trained to raise their cantering feet…now carrion on the plain. The cheese turned to chalk in her mouth.

"You had a mate, then, who died?" Thalas kept his distance.

"I *have* a mate," she growled, gripping the pieces of bread and cheese. He cocked his head. "I have a mate," she repeated, "and she'll find me. I won't be your slave forever."

Thalas put up his hands. "Your anger's just," he said, "but I only steer this ship. I can't even throw a lance. You're my guest. A slave to others' eyes, but to mine, a guest. Later, as you say, your mate…she…. Ah, you were with the Amazons. That's why you were dressed like a boy." He looked at her. She met his eyes steadily. "Well," he said finally, "we'll see Crete by dawn. I leave you to your grieving." He ducked out of the cabin. Marpessa stared at the empty doorway.

The Cretan mountains were in front of them with the first light, but the sun was well overhead before they rode into the Gulf of Pseira. Outside the headland, raw wind whipped the sea muddy green, but as they passed into the bay, six shades of blue caught the sunshine and sent it down into eelgrass and rocks spiny with sea urchins.

They skimmed by a long string of islands with inviting coves, but Thalas kept course on a flat shore between two rocky promontories. As they came under the lee of the western headland, the wind dropped, and the crew shouted down the sail, spinning the halyards into coils. Thalas kept the oarsmen rowing lightly until shallow water grounded them. The boat shuddered and stopped. Soon the whole fleet lay like beached porpoises, snouts dug into the sand.

The horses came out first, wobbly legged, and headed for the yellowing grass along the shore. Then the Trojan women staggered into the sunlight. They stood and blinked until two men herded them to a stream that fell over rocks onto the shore. Other men rolled out chariot wheels and fastened them to carts; the strongest horses were hostled into traces for the royal procession to Gournia.

Thalas handed Marpessa into his chariot and held out the reins. “I’m a seaman.” He shrugged. “I don’t want to embarrass myself in front of a horsebreaker.” She took the reins and flicked the horses into a trot. Ahead, Agamemnon’s chariot sprayed dust at them; behind, the king’s followers fell into line. On the shore, the crews continued to pile up battlegear and plunder.

The chariots jolted over heaved stones. Here and there yawed a hole deep enough to break an axle. Marpessa, watching the road, caught only glimpses of the graceful valley that rolled in three directions to the hills. The road curled around a low hill taking the procession toward the sun dipping behind square, white houses piled on a rock. Marpessa guided her team into the town's shadow and gave them over to a waiting boy. Agamemnon and Cassandra were already climbing a long flight of steps. Shuttered houses lined the steep street; except for the boy below and a grizzled man bowing and beckoning them on, there was no one in sight.

The palace, also shuttered, fronted onto a wide court. Steps gaped where flagstones were broken. The grimy facade held the charred outline of the flight to the second floor; the stairs lay in the rubble in the court below. The guide led the procession around to another stepped street that took them to the top of the ridge and the uppermost floor of the palace. Here one face and then another appeared, peeking at them like rabbits from a shattered warren. The guide bowed and let them pass into the fire-lit banquet hall.

Marpessa left when the singing began. She had listened to Agamemnon's bluster and the Cretans' servility, the honeyed wine turning to vinegar in her mouth. But the bard's voice extolling Greek heroism dug into her like a haw too thorny to pass. She slipped into the shadows and felt her way along the wall until a doorway let her out into the night. To the west, silhouettes of mountains jutted into the twilight; to the east, hills gave way to a range of peaks that stretched across the island to the other sea. Below her, the gulf waters glowed silver against the sprawling black headlands of the coast.

"This is the Troy of your grandchildren's time." Thalas held out a handful of ripe figs. "You left your venison. Maybe your appetite's better out here." She took a fig and bit into it. He leaned against a rail, watching her.

"Agamemnon's father sacked this city. I suppose my father swung a sword, too. Or maybe it was our fathers' fathers. Anyway, these Gournians have never amounted to much since then. Most of them got tired of fighting and took to the hills. Easier to live simply and grub food from the earth. Those who stayed, you can see, don't have the gumption to rebuild what was destroyed."

Marpessa narrowed her eyes. It would take more than gumption to rebuild a city raided by pirates year after year. This city had never had walls. The Gournians must have been at peace until the Greeks took to the seas. No wonder they hid behind shutters. She glared at Thalas.

"Why do you Greeks make war?"

He folded his hairy arms over his chest. "It's what we do best. Ask Agamemnon why we came to Troy, and he'll tell you his brother's honor had to be avenged. We made war for a noble cause: no foreigner can abuse Greek hospitality and sleep safely. But the truth is, we like to fight. We're good at it. And we get a lot from it, too. The fishing rights in the straits belong to Greece now. Trojan gold and silver will more than pay for the ships we lost. And the dead? There's always a new generation eager to fight. Not to mention the linen mills; who'd run them if we didn't bring back slaves?"

His voice was matter-of-fact, as if he were watching a school of smelt slide under a hull.

"And you? Why do *you* make war?"

He let the question hang in the night for a moment. Then, softly, "I don't make war. My king tells me to sail my boat. If I didn't do it, he'd get someone else and I'd rot in a dungeon. They're going to sack cities anyway; I might as well feel the wind in my face."

The sky had darkened enough for the evening star to push its steady glow earthward. A shore breeze sent shivers up Marpessa's back.

"What are you going to do with me?"

"Well, I thought for now we might go back down to the shore. They won't miss us here, and I think we both prefer sleeping under the stars. Then tomorrow, why don't you cut the yearlings from the herd, and we'll set up a training corral. You could teach me something about horses. If you like, I'll show you a few tricks of the sea. There's good red mullet in this gulf. Squid, too. As long as we're here for the winter, we might as well do what we do best." He hunched his shoulders and half-smiled at her.

Why fight him? thought Marpessa and followed him down the steps.

They built the corral out of willow saplings. The men of the fleet muttered when she first rode into the grazing herd, cutting the young ones away; Thalas silenced them with a jut of his chin. After that, they gave the corral wide berth.

Each day, as the sun rolled from horizon to overhead, Thalas netted fish from the bay while Marpessa taught her charges to step lightly and hold their heads high. Days when Thalas filled his fish basket early, he'd join her at the corral, heave himself onto whichever mare had wandered close by and let himself be paced, too. Some days he'd ask a question and learn more than he thought his head would hold.

"What makes a horse best? How can you tell when it's so young?"

Marpessa slipped the halter off a dun-colored colt and

slapped him on the flank. The colt eyed her to make sure he was really free to go, then bolted toward the herd. She walked to a three-year-old, ran her hand down the reddish foreleg and lifted the hoof. "Well," she said, "let's start here. See how the frog is thick and the hoof itself high? Makes her hooves ring like cymbals." She dropped the foot and rubbed the fetlock. "Here she's flexible, so she won't get inflamed on a long march—but not so low and springy that she'll get hurt when she gallops over clods and stones." Her hand slid up the leg. "Her shank-bone's thick; the flesh over it's thin. That means the back sinew'll hold tight." She clucked at the mare. "Watch her knees while she walks. See how flexible they are? Not likely to stumble, no matter what kind of stones you're running over." She clapped her hands, and the mare stood still. She caressed the breastbone. "Broad chest, see? Handsome and strong, and her neck rises like a game-cock's. The head? Narrow jawbone, sensitive mouth. And look at her face: eyes prominent but not bulgy, nostrils wide-open, small ears." She kissed the tip of the nose and held out a palmful of cheese. "Oh, what a beauty you are!" The mare drew her lips back, and curled her tongue around the chunk. Marpessa moved alongside her and slapped her withers. "Good seat, you can see, and the double loin makes her soft to ride. Solid quarters mean a lighter gallop; and her buttocks, see how they separate under her tail? Means her gait'll be proud. Ah, my little Starface, you really are a beauty." She hopped lightly and swung her leg over the broad back. "And those bastards, I'm glad they knew it." She turned to Thalas. "Throw a bridle on that dapple over there, and I'll give you another lesson."

Thalas fumbled the bit into the dapple's mouth. "Well, Spotty, she outclasses me by a long shot, but take me anyway so I can learn something new."

As Thalas took to the ways of horses, so Marpessa entered the world of ships and the sea. Solid oak, she learned, keeled the longships, and blackthorn made its stempost strong for ramming. Pitch was not enough to hold off barnacles, so copper sheathed the liveworks. On the ram-beaked prow, the unblinking eye warded off evil.

She learned about smaller craft, too. She helped Thalas shape pine ribs for his fishing coracle. They cleaned the skins of thirty hares and stretched them over the frame. He showed her how to step the mast and hang the sails on the yardarm. Her first day out, he set her at the steering oar and taught her how to catch wind in the sail or spill it if the gust was too hard.

She decided a boat, like a horse, had a mind of its own. Yoked to the wind, though, it could be bent to her will so long as she read the sky well. Dark wisps along the horizon, she learned, foretold angry waves carrying a storm into the bay.

On solstice eve, the wind dropped to a sough. "Look," said Thalas, "it's like this every year. We Greeks say Aeolus, who carries the winds, calms the waves on these short days so the kingfisher can build her nest on the water. He gives her seven days, then rouses the storms again."

She looked at him. "We Amazons call him Aeolus, too. We say Mama Thetis, our mother, consorted with him on just such a calm sea. Out of their mating came the first Amazon."

"A common god, Greeks and Amazons? But Thetis is only a sea nymph to us and Achilles' mother at that. I suppose that tells you all you need to know about us Greeks."

"Some of you," she said and laid her hand in his.

On the fourth of the kingfisher days Marpessa saw Cassandra instead of Thalas waiting at the corral gate.

"Marpessa, be my friend."

"What else would I be, if not your friend?" Marpessa opened the gate to let her charges frisk off to the herd. "First an embrace. Then tell me your mind."

They held each other, Cassandra's bones light in Marpessa's embrace. Then, arms linked, they walked to the shore. Thalas' coracle was pulled high, its hull not yet damp from the morning sea. Marpessa's eyes swept the shoreline, but she saw only the crews stuffing flax into the seams of the beached ships. At the water's edge, Cassandra stretched out her arms. A seagull swung low, almost settling on her palm, then beat its wings skyward. Marpessa picked up a smooth black stone and rubbed her cheek with it.

"I'm dreaming again," said Cassandra. "When we first came to Crete, I slept deeply, but since the sun turned in its course, the dreams have begun again." She stooped and let a handful of beach pebbles slide through her fingers. "D'you remember the dreams I told you, about the wild dogs and the peacocks? I dream them again, but now the biggest dog carries a peahen, unharmed, in its mouth. The way to the lair is clear, but as the beast stands there waiting to be greeted by its bitch, a cypress falls and crushes dog and peahen."

Marpessa continued to rub her cheek for a long moment. Then she swung her arm; the smooth black stone sailed high before it dropped into the waveless water. "And we peahens," she said through her teeth, "are spared the fires of Troy only to die in a foreign land."

"No," Cassandra caught her arm, "not we. Only I will

die with him. The falling cypress starts a wild pheasant. Two speckled eggs are in its nest. You won't die there, Marpessa; Trojan ways can live in you." Marpessa lifted her face to the grey sky and closed her eyes. A single tear squeezed through her lashes and dried before it reached her mouth. Cassandra stroked her arm. "Or Amazon ways. I forget. You're an Amazon now." Cassandra laid her cheek on Marpessa's shoulder. "I didn't come to make you grieve, but to be with you. Be my friend."

The winds began again, and still the fishing coracle lay dry on the shore. The first mate shrugged. "You never know. He might go off for days—or weeks. He's like that." A captain glared at her. "If he's gone, so what? It's no loss to us." A Trojan woman finally gave her a clue. "One of the princes lost his women throwing bones. He thought he'd replenish his stock with Cretans and went raiding. When he brought them back, your Thalas fought him hard. I think he took some horses and escorted them back to their villages." Marpessa counted the herd and, sure enough, the dapple and six others were gone. She mounted a bay and rode into the morning sun.

She found him on a ledge dug into a rocky hillside overlooking the whitecapped sea. Above, paved terraces marched up to a temple. Wild goats nibbled junipers on the sacred slope; a flock of crows lined the bull horns crowning the sanctuary. Among the pebbles at her feet, Marpessa spotted a clay dung beetle, a plea from a shepherd for a good lambing or a fisherman for a good run of mackerel.

Thalas looked up, his face drawn. “Welcome.” His voice was barely audible over the wind. She hunkered next to him and rolled the dung beetle between her fingers. He pointed to a solitary gull beating its wings hard against the wind yet seeming to stand still over the broad and empty sea. As she watched, the gull stopped its frantic flail and sailed backward with the wind toward Egypt, then turned again and flew hard to stay in the same place.

“Beating against the wind is lonely,” said Thalas. “Times I wish my heart could thump with the spilling of another man’s guts.” Marpessa settled onto a curve of the ledge and swung her feet over the dropoff. Thalas stared out at the gull. “When I was a boy, my brother punched me and jeered, but I never liked the feel of flesh on my fist. When I was sixteen, my father set me to oversee the spinners in the family linen mill. I couldn’t make the whip crack. When he found out about the extra dippers of barley I gave the pregnant women, he set me on one of his ships to become a trader. Surprise for both of us–I love the wind and the sea. Especially the night sky. I took an astrologer from Cyprus to Syria once who told me about the sacred pull of the stars on our lives. I believe him, I can feel it.”

Marpessa tried to read the weathered face as if it were a cloudbank. The man had something to say; she would wait.

“Well, my business wasn’t in the stars; it was in the ports. But I like trading, too. Every island in this sea is different. The speech is different, different the way they paint their boats. I like to take a hold full of my father’s linenwear to Naxos and trade it for speckled obsidian. The stone bowls from Crete go to Anatolia for lapis, the lapis to Egypt for painted ostrich eggs. Scarabs, too, bigger than the one you've got there, and covered with gold and amethyst."

The gull dropped suddenly, hovered over a breaking wave, and then settled onto a swell. "I'm glad you came for me," continued Thalas. "I've missed human company. The Cretans scurry past me with their eyes to the ground. They start like hares if I say hello."

"Why should they guess you're different from the Agamemnons of your race?"

"Well, it didn't matter before. Seagulls and stars used to be company enough."

"Before...?"

Thalas stared out at the gull, struggling into the wind again. "It isn't true, what I told you. I didn't have to join this war. I could have stayed in Anatolia...except an army of Hittites was burning cities there. I got caught in a storm off Thera, broke my steering oar, lost my mast. When I got home, I found my brother overseeing the laying of that solid oak keel. I watched the stern- and stemposts rise up, the ribs curve, the crossbeams join the ribs. They planked her and rigged her, and...and I wanted to see how she sailed. I love a well-built ship the way you love a well-bred horse."

Marpessa rubbed her dung beetle. Behind them a whinny was answered by a snort; her bay had found the hobbled dapple grazing a bed of thyme.

Thalas turned to her and caught her hand. "I missed you," he said. "I wanted you."

It was her turn to look out at the struggling gull. She saw a brown Amazon body flying with the gull, and it made her own body ache for holding. A seedling might be a sapling before lovepears would ripen again. Cassandra told her to carry Amazon ways inside her. Why not an Amazon child?

She stood up and balanced herself on one foot. The gull turned again to ride the wind. A wave crashing below swallowed her sigh. “There must be a bed of moss under that cypress over there. I came because I missed you.” She pulled Thalas to his feet. They turned from the rocky shore and let the wind push them toward night.

Exile

Mycenean Greece
seven years after the fall of Troy
seven years of slavery

"I've come to see my daughter."

Thalas leaned against the doorway of the counting room. Behind him, a hundred wooden shuttles lurched through a hundred hanging looms. Marpessa, on her knees in front of a wooden bench, drew a barley sign on the clay tablet in front of her and marked it thirty. She didn't look up. "The last time you saw your daughter, she crawled and babbled. Now she dances and tells stories. Do you think she remembers you?"

Thalas shifted his weight and winced at the pain that connected his knee to his big toe. "You're right to chide me. I'd tell you the winds were unfavorable, but you'd know better. Come on, leave your accounts and walk to the spring with me. I'll tell you why I'm tardy."

Marpessa dug the stylus into the clay and gouged out "weavers." "That's how much each woman behind you is allotted," she rasped. Thalas had to lean forward to catch her mutters over the clatter of the looms. "Thirty minas of barley. Even the pregnant ones. Your kinfolk need so much for themselves and so much more to keep the royal army in spears. Walk to the spring with you? I think your nephew has other plans." She nodded at the approaching overseer.

"Uncle!" The overseer stepped into the counting room and gave Thalas a quick hug. "Don't slow her down. She's fast, but you should see the farmers lined up out back." He turned to Marpessa. "Have you finished those allotments yet? Stack them over there and then bring your counting board around to the loading scales." He leaned close to Thalas and lowered his voice. "She's a jewel, this girl. Her figures are clear and she never makes a mistake. Don't cross her, though, or she's a vixen. No playing around after dark, either; she'll eat you alive." He straightened his back and clapped Thalas' shoulder. "You'll come for dinner. Father's expecting you. He's got ideas for a new trade route." The overseer bustled out.

Marpessa laid down her stylus and laughed at the scowl that rolled over Thalas' face.

"You never learn, do you? You sail away in your ship. You treat your crew as if you were all brothers together, off on some bold adventure. When you come back, you've forgotten how some of us are slaves and some of you are owners. All right. I won't blame you for your family's starvation allotments, but you *can* tell me why you let your daughter grow up without you. I'll be busy counting flax bundles until sundown. You'll eat lamb at your brother's table. But tomorrow's Jug Day, and the mill is closed. The mummers play in the morning. We aren't going to stay for the drinking contests, so come and find us when the procession gets to the square. We'll all slip away to the spring together while the rest of the city swills."

Most days Mycenae was grey. The boulders of the city walls matched the grey clouds that blanketed the mountains behind; grey mists hung in the ravines. To the south, the Argolian plain stretched sunny and green all the way to the sea while grey Mycenae crouched on its crag demanding tribute.

Wine Jug Day was different; it was sunny by order of the king. The gods were absent; you couldn't even swear to one to trade a mule. Chewed buckthorn leaves were supposed to keep the ghosts away, and, if that didn't work, the mummers' insults would send them flying back to their graves. After the first two craters of wine, the complaints of murdered souls no longer mattered. By the time the queen of the marshes was mating with the masked god of the vine, none of it mattered: neither the bloody death of Agamemnon nor the bumbling rule of his cousin with his queen.

It mattered to Marpessa. Not the king's butchering, but the unsung death of Cassandra. At the spring, water bubbled out of a rockpile and fed a pool ringed by elderbushes. Elderblossoms meandered across the water and fetched up against lily pads; the only sounds were the gurgles of the spring and the occasional croak of a frog. It was her place for remembering.

"My heart aches for her daily." Marpessa leaned against a stump and watched her daughter Lampeto, ankle-deep and peering into the pool. Thalas clasped his hairy arms around his knees and listened. "Cassandra was my first home, you know. She let me go and she welcomed me back. She was my family. But for a jealous queen she would have been my family here in this dreary city of yours. She didn't crave Agamemnon's bed; she didn't deserve his death. She saw it coming, you know. She dreamed it in Crete. She saw it in every sooty shearwater banking a wave. When the ships sailed into the harbor down there, she saw it in a sparrow hawk hovering over a hemlock. Her speech was all ravings as the wagon carried us from the harbor to Agamemnon's palace, but when the queen appeared to welcome her husband home, she spoke to me clearly. I can still hear her voice in my ears. 'Her fury covets his blood and mine,' she said. 'In death be my friend.' She didn't speak again."

Thalas shifted and waited for more. Lampeto broke into the remembering. "Mama, look!" She opened her cupped hands to reveal a peeper. "It jumped right in! Is it a baby? Can I keep it?"

"It's a brave little adventurer, isn't it? No, if it were a baby, it'd have a tail. It only gets that big. It probably has babies of its own, so you can't keep it or they'll miss their mama."

Lampeto opened her hands, and the peeper sailed into the pond. "Bye, now. Say hello to your babies for me."

Eyes on his daughter, Thalas slaked his own thirst for family. "I wish I were more a father to her, more family to you."

"Your ship's your family. I grew up fatherless in Troy, you know. And Amazons don't recognize their children's fathers as family. I miss you when you're away so long, but it's my Amazon kin-kith that I wait for. You know that."

"Have you had any message from her?"

Marpessa touched Thalas' elbow and pointed to the top of a pine bent sideways with the weight of a blue heron. "Graceful isn't he, for all his size. But Lampeto doesn't forgive him; he rid this pond of every frog last summer." The heron stretched its wings and glided down to the pond. "No, no message. I feel her speaking to me from time to time, and two nights ago she was in my dreams, but no other message. Without a ship, it's a long distance, isn't it?"

"I ask because there's talk of an Amazon migration. A Phrygian who took passage on my ship last summer said the Amazons have left their river home."

Marpessa stiffened. "How did he know?"

"His brother's a royal courier, took a letter from his king begging help against the Hittites. He found the city deserted, only wild goats wandering the streets. It hadn't been attacked; the walls stood, not a stone broken. Just no one there."

The heron paused its stilted wade; Lampeto shook her fist. "You can't have my peeper!" she shouted. "She's faster than you. You can't catch her!"

Marpessa laid her cheek on her knee and watched the child and the heron glaring at each other. Thalas let his hand rest on her braid. "I thought you'd want to know more, so I found a cargo of figs bound for Sinope. It's close enough to Themiscyra, I thought someone could tell me. I asked a few questions, and they brought me a bandy-legged fellow, a grimy Gargarensian who used to mine ore. His Greek was vile, but his tongue was loose enough after a few craters of wine. He babbled about the Hittites, how they'd come swarming through the mountain pass—thousands, tens of thousands. He and his family fled into the ore tunnels. I pressed him about the Amazons. 'Oh, they were gone long before that,' he said. 'They left after the bones of their queen came back from Troy.' Then he wailed on about the Hittites. I left him and picked up a cargo of iron my brother can turn a profit with."

Marpessa's muscles tightened. "Why did you wait to tell me?" She shook her braid, shook Thalas' hand away from her. "Didn't you ask him where they'd gone? What good is knowing they're gone and not knowing where?"

He rubbed his hand. She drooped. "I'm sorry. It's the first I've heard of the Amazons since your ship left Troy, and it tells me nothing I want to know. Did he say which direction they took?"

"I'm sorry. I wanted to tell you sooner, but I couldn't talk with all those clattering looms. I asked the fellow where they'd gone, but he slipped into the dialect of the coast. The word he used might have meant 'old home' or maybe 'ancient grounds.' Anyway, I don't see this as bad news. If the queen's bones arrived before they left, then your Melanippe's filial duty was done; she'd turn to her kin-kith duty—to you. As you say, it's a long journey. She could take a ship, of course, but you told me Amazons never sail. Thrace is a wild country. It's been only seven years since we all left Troy; even ships get blown off course. They say Odysseus has yet to be seen in Ithaca, but his wife turns away suitors; she's certain he'll return."

Marpessa accepted the rebuke in silence. The heron flapped its wings and flew away. Shadows lengthened over the water. Thalas stretched. "The revelers must be off to the marshes by now. I caught some trout yesterday, left a string of them over there by the rocks. Shall we eat and watch the stars come out?"

Marpessa nodded. She watched him build a fire, clean the fish, and spit them over the coals. She, too, had news that waited a quiet moment. While the mullet skins reddened, she took a deep breath and spoke.

"I decided to give Lampeto a sister."

It was Thalas' turn to stiffen, but he only lifted the spit off the fire. Lampeto, who had abandoned the frogs, leaned over and patted her mother's tummy. "Baby's in a cradle going flippity flip," she chanted softly. Thalas pulled the fish off the spit and folded each one into a grape leaf. If Marpessa wanted him to speak his thoughts, she knew she would have to wait. She broke the silence herself.

"Your family tolerates me only because of you. Of course, they're happy enough with my accounts, but away from my stylus I'm invisible. They fussed when Lampeto was born because babies are to fuss over. Now that she's older, she's invisible, too. I wait for Melanippe; but a kin-kith is only a mate. I want my own family, too." She bit through the mottled skin into succulent white flesh.

Thalas swallowed his fish and wiped his mouth. "And I can't be your family, can I? Even if I stay here. I'm only the good friend you see from time to time. Tell me, at least, who the father is." Lampeto grinned at him and wiped her fingers on his leggings. He invited her into his lap and held her loosely.

"He's a farmer for one of the landholders around here. That's how I met him; he brought flax to the mill. He hasn't come since last full moon, though. He doesn't even know I'm swelling. He doesn't need to, either; the child's for me and Lampeto." She hunched forward and touched Thalas' hand. "I waited for you, you know. I'd have preferred your blood in this child-to-be. But we heard about so many storms and so many shipwrecks and so many sailors going off to make Cyprus or Syria their home. I didn't know when I'd see you again."

Thalas took her hand and held it as if it were Lampeto's peeper. The child yawned and snuggled deeper into his lap. A light flashed on the mountain above them.

"Look up there!" said Marpessa. "There're fires in the mountains these days; times are urgent. I think that's where this baby's father has gone."

Two more flashes were answered by two on the mountain across.

"Fires on the mountains?" echoed Thalas, as he watched another set of flares.

Marpessa talked into the night, and Thalas learned that the fires on the mountains were kept burning by men who called themselves brigands for freedom. Fierce men, heroes in the countryside, they pledged to trample a way of life that had chafed their kind for a thousand years. They rode into villages demanding tribute, and mothers held up babies for their blessings. If they happened on a boy driving his father's ox, they might take both boy and ox to their lair, the ox to eat, the boy to make a man of. If they chanced on a young woman dipping water at a wayside spring, they might take her gold necklace and ring to trade for swords and knives, and if the ring didn't slide easily in their grasp, they might cut off a finger. The woman would bleed, but she might carry her wound proudly, a badge for freedom.

"They welcome this crumbling kingdom," Marpessa told Thalas. "They cheered Agamemnon's death and even more the royal squabbling that followed. They see in nature's rampages a sign from the gods for their side. Just after Agamemnon was killed, an earthquake took down the main bridge. We were ordered to sacrifice, an ox from each mill, and the bridge was rebuilt. The day the masons finished, another quake shattered it. We sacrificed again, and this time the earth shook before the next bridge was half-built. After that we heard no more about sacrificing or bridges. We take another road. The brigands told us to celebrate.

"In these years since the king's death, we've suffered flood and drought as well as earthquake, and with every disaster, men leave the fields and go up into the mountains. We were busy at the mill yesterday, but some days the line at the loading dock is short, and the looms close down at noon. Our allotments are short those days, too.

The weavers say they are looking to the brigands for our salvation, but I don't know that I trust those men. They leave their families with nothing, sometimes not even a donkey for hauling."

Thalas listened in silence and pondered his homeland's disorder. "The world isn't the way it was," he said finally. "Is there somewhere safe I can take you? Sicily? A new start for us all?"

Marpessa brushed an elderberry blossom from the sleeping Lampeto's braid. "And how would my kin-kith find me there?" she said quietly.

A log broke, scattering sparks and ashes. Lampeto turned in her sleep. The flashing had stopped, and the mountains behind them were dark.

Marpessa swelled through a long summer drought. When the winter rains finally struck the parched earth, the baby came out screaming. He was not a sister for Lampeto. Marpessa stared at his maleness and then at his howling face; she stopped his mouth with her breast. By the time he toddled, the flashing on the twin peaks had spread all along the mountain range. Fields planted went unharvested, the loading scales were empty, and the mill looms hung threadless. Thalas' ship, half-full of cargo, lifted anchor and sailed.

Marpessa kept watch on the northern mountain pass where one day, surely, Melanippe would appear. Out of habit as much as faith, she marked each noontide watching. She was startled, but not surprised, when a hoarse voice finally called to her in the familiar coastal dialect.

"Marpessa! I've come for you!"

CHOICE

Mycenean Greece
ten years after the fall of Troy
a ten-year-old girl, a yearling boy

Melanippe had tales to tell: The grieving journey from Troy to Themiscyra. The leave-taking as the city emptied. The raft-ride over churning waters into Thrace and the endless plains, forests, and always one more mountain range. Burning cities, brigands at every pass, pirates guarding the ports. Melanippe had tales...but she didn't tell them. Through long evenings at the spring, she listened to Marpessa's stories; she carved a monkey puppet for Lampeto; she made a shell rattle for the baby Batis. Her eyes missed nothing, but her mouth opened only for food and love.

She was taller than Marpessa remembered her, and leaner. A still-red scar creased her eyebrow and hollows rounded her eyes. She moved like a cat stalking ducks.

Marpessa had honed her patience with Thalas. From time to time, as evening lengthened the shadows at the spring, she broke the silence with a question.

"You buried your mother's bones?"

"I buried my mother's bones."

"By the river?"

"By the river." A long pause. "In the tomb of the warriors, where the water pours from the rocks."

Another evening, after roasted partridge, "Why did they leave Themiscyra?"

"There were signs."

"Where did they go?"

"Home."

"Home? Themiscyra is home."

"Home-before-Themiscyra. The place of the ancients."

Wait, Marpessa counselled herself. Wait.

The wait was rewarded with a song.

Black clouds gathering, white rocks wandering
pitched on a soundless shore.
Then off go the mare-kin riding the east wind,
the wormwooded plain be a home once more.

Marpessa tried to make meaning of the song. Surely black clouds gathering is a storm, she thought. But can rocks wander? And seashores are never without sound: waves break, gulls call. Was the song like Cassandra's riddles? But it seemed to tell a past instead of a future.

Lampeto interrupted her ponderings. "Mama, Melanippe! A tortoise shell! I found it under an elderberry. Look how big it is! The tortoise who lived here must have been a great-grandma."

Melanippe took the shell and turned it over and over in her hands. She smiled at Lampeto. "A gift from the netherworld," she said. "May I borrow it for singing?"

Lampeto nodded and watched Melanippe scrape the undershell with her knife. When the inside was smooth, Melanippe chipped two holes into either end of the shell. Thread undone from her shirt became string to stretch from hole to hole. She plucked one string, then the other.

She retied a knot. She plucked again and tied again. She continued plucking and tying until the two tones that came from the plucking sounded both one note and two distinct notes. She leaned back and closed her eyes, plucking one string and then the other. A hollow rhythmic drone marched from the tortoise shell into the evening air. Lampeto peered into the shell, awed that her find could make such sounds.

"Sing to us," urged Marpessa, and Melanippe sang.

Melanippe, daughter of Thetis,
Melanippe, born a black foal.

She sang about the wormwood-studded steppe of Scythia and the broad river that flows into the sea. She sang about winter ice and spring break-up and ice floes big as boulders that wander out to sea. She sang about sailors who came once to raid horses, and Amazons who followed them onto their ships, and sailors who fell under Amazon blades. She sang about the ships, sails set, carrying Amazons like ice floes away from their first homeland and out to sea. The song reached into the night. When the last note had drifted across the pond and faded, Marpessa understood the riddle.

Migration after migration had taken the Amazons eventually to Themiscyra, but the riddle-song had traveled with them to remind them that one day, when ice floes reached as far as the southern shore of the Blackfog Sea, the daughters of Thetis would return to their ancient home in Scythia. Marpessa folded her hand over Melanippe's still on the tortoise-shell lyre. "We'll go ourselves and find them, yes?"

Melanippe set down the lyre and put both arms around Marpessa. "Soon," she whispered and kissed the ear she whispered into.

Lampeto had fallen asleep, her arm tucked under her head. But the boy was awake and, mouth rounded like a lamprey's, he reached for Marpessa's nipple.

With the lyre to help her set speech to song, Melanippe seemed more the young Amazon Marpessa had fallen in love with. She took to poking her head through the counting-room window for a mid-morning kiss, laughing at Marpessa's fear of being caught. She coaxed a royal stablehand into letting her exercise two of the king's horses and made a training schedule for Lampeto. One morning she slung the boy in a pouch across her chest—"It's no good for him to breathe linen dust, and he'll get the feel of the horses"—and carried him as if he were her own. Most evenings by the spring, she sang, but from time to time she talked about her travels to Mycenae.

"There's a war going on"—Melanippe's eyes reflected the fireglow, and her hands waved in front of her—"bigger than we saw at Troy. It isn't kings killing kings anymore. The royal marauders are tasting their own medicine from an enemy they can't even see."

Marpessa shivered and drew Lampeto closer, but Lampeto wanted to talk about riding to the land of the Amazons. "We'll have to follow deer trails and stay away from cities. We'll have to stay away from the mountains, too, because the brigands might catch us. I can jump onto my horse running now, and I can draw my bow while

I'm riding—today I made three bull's eyes in a row. Melanippe says I'm ready."

"Do you know how to get to where our people have settled?" Marpessa asked Melanippe.

"We'll find their trail when we get to Thrace. Cleite said to follow the rim of the Blackfog Sea. We should cross four great rivers, two far from each other and two that come together in a lake. After the lake, there's a caravan trail through wormwood and vetch. When we reach a broad river that pours into the sea, our new home will be waiting for us."

"We'll go soon?"

"I found a brigand who'll trade three mares if I can get him twenty swords from the king's arsenal. I've been scouting for a week now. The guards are always drunk by midnight. You should be weaning the boy. He'll go to his father."

Marpessa swallowed her gasp. She had seen herself riding away with Melanippe a thousand times, yet she had never seen the boy left behind. She knew Amazon law: boys grow up with their fathers. But what father did Batis have? The man who'd seeded her still lit fires on the mountains; she wasn't sure she'd know his face.

The boy gurgled and let her nipple fall from his mouth. Marpessa held him against her shoulder and thumped his back. Her mouth tightened into a line. Tomorrow, she thought, I'll start the weaning tomorrow.

Full moons passed. The season turned. At harvest time, at the dark of the moon, Melanippe was gone three nights running. Marpessa paced the hard-packed floor from cradle to window to cradle again. She wished for Cassandra. Someone who loved her and knew her. Someone to talk to about the too-soon separation, not to advise her—she'd made her choice—but to listen to her heart. She willed Cassandra's image by the fire.

A tap at the door made her jump. "Cassandra!" she breathed, but the head that poked round the door was a different friend.

"Thalas! I thought you'd gone for good."

"I've been helping my brother set up mills in Sicily. He's planning to transport the loom-women, but not before next spring. I came to warn you, so you could make your own plans. Have you heard from Melanippe?" Marpessa rubbed her forehead against his chest. All she could speak was his name. He rested his chin on her head. "You're crying. Bad news? Tell me."

Marpessa pushed herself away from him and brushed her cheeks with both hands. "No. Yes. Melanippe's here. We're leaving as soon as she gets horses." Her shoulders drooped. "Come and sit. I'll poke the fire and mull some wine."

As she turned to fetch the jug, she squeezed her eyes to keep tears from falling. Melanippe was kin-kith, not to be betrayed, but Thalas was a friend, waiting to be what a friend can be.

"She left her people to come for me," she began, as if that could explain the choice. "I love her. She loves me. We sit together at the spring, and sometimes I feel we're one creature seeing with four eyes; other times I feel strong in the world alone, and yet her presence is all around me. We look at each other, and I feel forever."

She pulled the wine jug from the fire and poured a cup for Thalas. She put her cup to her lips, then set it aside.

"But the world's not just the two of us. For me, the world is either with the Greeks or with the Amazons. Greece is crumbling. Everyone knows it now, even your brother. That's why he's moving his mills to Sicily. Anyone who can barter shipspace is fleeing. The brigands are everywhere. This city's going to burn.

"Melanippe says the danger is less if we leave before the burning. As soon as she gets horses, we'll be gone. The Amazons have settled on some wild plain north of the Blackfog Sea, and we're going to find them."

She glanced over at the silent cradle and twisted a strand of hair around her fingers. She looked at the door, the window, and, finally, Thalas. "I love those women, you know that; my heart longs to be with them. But there, in that basket is my flesh and blood, and he's the barter for Amazonia." She stopped, out of breath. Bile rose in her throat. She pressed her fist against her mouth to drive it back. The cradle creaked as Batis shifted in sleep.

"We used to sing a song in Troy. Not at the palace, but in the huts in the marshes. About building a bridge across the Scamander. The river god demands a sacrifice, and the master builder offers his wife. She has an unweaned baby, a boy like Batis, I imagine. The master builder, her husband, tricks her into going down into the foundation, then throws stones on top of her. She begs him first for her life, then she asks him to put a window in the foundation so she can offer her breast to her baby."

Thalas, his broad hands resting on his knees, said

nothing. His eyes followed hers to the cradle and met them on the way back.

"You'll ask me to stay here," she continued, "go to Sicily next spring, raise the boy and the girl with your family. I know you'll mean it, too. You forget we're slaves. You've never treated me like a slave, but your family never lets me forget. Lampeto will go into the mill next year and she's not half-grown. Shall I teach her to write so she can kneel in front of a clay tablet all day instead of standing at a loom? Kneeling or standing, the allotment's the same. And who knows if your brother's mills will last to spring? The brigands may have burned them by solstice. It's different for the boy. If the brigands take him, they'll see him as a future warrior; they'll give him goat testicles for courage."

She poked the fire. Outside, a tree limb creaked against a roof tile.

"I've decided. One of the weavers will take Batis. Melanippe and Lampeto and I will find our way to our people on the wormwood steppe. My nipple will ache for his teeth, but an ache is only an ache. My heart, well...a heart can love in pieces, can't it? With his goat testicles, he'll get a bit of my heart to make him gentle, too."

A pebble rolled in the courtyard. Marpessa cocked an ear; Thalas looked to the door. It opened a crack, and Melanippe, elbow cradled against her chest, slipped inside.

"The horses are by the fig tree!" she whispered. "We go tonight! The guards were drunk but they still raised a ruckus." She took in Thalas by the fire. "Is that the boy's father? Good. He can take him now. We leave before dawn. Can you wrap this for me?"

The wound was shallow, the bleeding had stopped. Marpessa stared at her. Thalas was the one who tore a strip from his cloak, soaked it with water, and washed the elbow clean. He wrapped it carefully and tore another strip to bind it. Marpessa knelt beside the cradle.

"I'm not Batis' father," he said to Melanippe. "I'm Lampeto's." He turned to Marpessa. "I'll take the boy, though, if you need me to. Tell me where this weaver lives." He swallowed. "Or, if you let me, I'll care for him myself."

Melanippe ducked into the shadows and began tucking bread and onions into a pouch. Marpessa ran her finger along the cradle's edge, started to reach in and touch the boy, then drew back as if from a flame.

"I'll care for him myself," repeated Thalas. "I've got a house now in Sicily. My own, not my brother's. The sea air hurts my leg these days; I need time on land. Let me take Batis. I haven't been a father to Lampeto; let me be one to him."

Marpessa, dry-eyed, stood up. She walked to the corner where Melanippe was packing. "Take him," she said, not turning. "Raise him as slave or son. I am an Amazon. I have no sons." She took a leather flask from its peg on the wall and squatted next to the water jug.

There were snickers when Thalas appeared on the shore, a baby swaddled to his chest, but his crew knew him as an odd duck and went on loading linen bales into the hold. Thalas felt a surge of pride each time the boy, his boy now, shifted against him. The burden warmed him. Here was his family.

Mid-morning the boy started wailing. At first a

sniffle, then hiccoughs, then a long, low wail rising to a piercing scream. Thalas unbundled him, washed his dirtied bottom in the shallow water at the shore, and offered him a milk-soaked rag. Batis backhanded the rag and screamed louder. Thalas dipped it in the milk jug again. Batis flailed. A crew member called over the rail, "Toss him into the sea and let a sea nymph nurse him!" Another shipmaster paused nearby. "You're taking on crew a bit young, aren't you?" Thalas tried to stroke the boy to calm him, but Batis arched his back and beat his tiny fists in the air.

A herd of goats rounded onto the shore, behind them a pair of ragged herders. The bleating blended with the baby's howls. One of the herders, an old woman, called out to him. "It wants a teat, son! What have you done with its mother?"

Thalas held the baby at arms' length. "She's gone! Can you help?"

The old woman brought her stick down hard on the back of a straggling billy. Then she prodded a nanny away from the herd. She lurched over to Thalas, dragging one foot, and squatted in front of him. The nanny followed. The old woman took the screaming Batis and shoved him under the swollen udder. His open mouth found milk. The screaming stopped. "It wants a teat," she repeated.

When Batis had finished, the old woman drew him to her sunken chest and murmured a lullaby. "*Nani, nani, nani,*" she crooned, her voice clear as a thrush's. "May you grow into a cypress, son, may your branches spread from east to west." Batis snuggled and fell asleep.

"Will you sell me the nanny?"

The old woman squinted at him. "What's it worth to you?"

"A bundle of linen?"

"Linen for a goatherd." She spat. "Shall I sew myself a sail and sail my goats to market? What else have you got?"

"An amphora of wine. The sweet kind, from Laconia. Or oil. Pressed last harvest."

The old woman rubbed her nose. "One of each." She laid the sleeping Batis on a ledge and staggered to her feet. "One for each shoulder," she said, flexing her muscles.

Thalas called over to a crew member standing at the rail. "No need to gawk at a bartering. Toss us an oil and a wine."

Loaded, the herder shuffled away. Thalas picked up a loose rope and tied the nanny to a log. He knelt and touched the boy's forehead. "We'll manage, son," he whispered. "I'll learn this mothering, I swear it."

Marpessa found them both on board, curled together on the stern thwart, the nanny midships chewing seaweed. Thalas felt a shadow move through his dream and opened his eyes.

"I couldn't leave him," she said flatly. The night breeze lifted a lock on her forehead. "A seedling needs water. A baby needs his mother's milk."

Thalas disentangled himself from the boy and sat up. "Lampeto?"

"She wants to live where girls are free."

"Melanippe?"

"She'll forgive me." She leaned against the rail. A pair

of gulls bobbed into the moon's path across the water. Thalas joined her, careful to leave space enough between them. She rubbed her breast. Why? she thought. Why do I have to choose? Love is precious, why does it cost so much? On the road, my nipples bled. Now my heart is bleeding. I grieve my son, or I grieve my daughter and lover. They can survive without my milch breasts. He can't. Is that a choice?

She stared at the gulls. With the pair were babies, eleven of them, no, an even dozen. They drifted toward the ship until they were almost in its shadow. "When your down turns to feathers," she whispered, "you'll be on your own." She turned to Thalas. "I'll find them," she said. "When my son doesn't need a mother, I'll be an Amazon again. Until then, my kin-kith will love me, my daughter will remember her mother."

Search

Sicily
twenty years after the fall of Troy
a ten-year-old boy, a mother leaving

The boy grew well in Sicily while Thalas, away from his ship, declined. Days he tended a vineyard terraced into the hillside behind the house; evenings he sat in a waterfront wine-house seeking news from the sea. He was gentle as always, but he rarely spoke to either mother or son.

In Greece, Marpessa had lived with only a chattering daughter for company, a life lonely but not difficult. In Sicily, life with a rambunctious son and a brooding man was lonely and unbearable. She urged Thalas back to his ship; by the time he mustered a crew, the sea to the east was closed to trade. He chose a western route. The leavetaking was painful for both.

"How far will you go?"

"At least to Iberia. There's tin there. If the winds are favorable, we'll go out through the pillars of Heracles onto the ocean river."

"Where the earth ends, they say. Aren't you afraid of being swept over the edge?"

"We'll hug the shore. If we go far enough north, there'll be amber to trade for." He looked down at a clamshell on the shore. "I haven't been a good father, after all, have I? I thought that's what I wanted, but I kept feeling the hills close around me. I'm sorry."

"You know what they say: a seaman's like a fish and dies out of water. I'm glad for us both that you're going. Don't worry about Batis; he's already attached himself to the smith next to the mill. He gets to blow the bellows sometimes."

"I'll miss you. I'll miss you both."

For Marpessa it was more than missing; she knew the goodbye was final. When Thalas returned, he would find only the boy; she herself would be north, north of the Blackfog Sea.

Pirates lay between her and Greece. She knew how to sail, though, and how to build a boat pirates might ignore. After that, she could turn peddler and sell whatever a farmer or brigand might need. Even in wartime, a peddler moves invisible through the land.

She built the coracle exactly the way she and Thalas had built the one in Crete: hareskins stretched over pine ribs, a cypress mast. The sail she pieced together with linen scraps from the mill. She made friends with Batis' smith; not only would he give the boy his future trade, he was her source of trove: kitchenware and spades for the farmers, dirks and axes for the brigands.

"What's a good woman like yourself want with dirks and axes?" he asked her.

"There's need of them in Greece. There aren't so many smiths there these days, and they like Sicilian forging."

He agreed to take on Batis as apprentice even though the boy was only half-grown. She took her treasures and stowed them around the mast.

Leaving her son was no easier than saying goodbye to Thalas even though he was taking on manners that made her eager to be done with mothering. "Water!" he'd call to her, his head thrown back and his mouth bold. The boldness would melt under her glare, and sheepishly he'd fetch his own. The next day he'd loose another command. Yet he rescued baby bluejays when they tumbled from their nests and he tended a grove of pomegranates for a neighbor, offering her the blushing fruit as if it were gold.

She waited until the fig leaves had unfurled and then traded her woman's gown for a short tunic and leggings. She bound her buxom breasts until they merged with her belly, glad that her girth made a fatty chest unnoticable. She cut her hair until it just reached her shoulder and matted the severed plait for a beard. Batis giggled as he watched her, but when she turned to him fully costumed, he staggered back.

"Mama! Where are you?" he shouted.

She kissed his forehead. "You'll be good, yes? You'll do exactly what the smith tells you and you'll eat well and grow tall as a cypress. When Thalas comes home, you'll kiss him for me. Help me carry these to my boat."

From out in the bay, he looked small and lonely. Twice Marpessa's hand almost swung the steering oar, but she held her course. One turning back was enough; her life was waiting. A last look caught the smith bending down to the boy and the two, hand in hand, walking away from the bay, from her. May you fare well, she breathed, and looked toward Greece.

She landed in a shallow cove with sandbars all around. Pylos, she reckoned, lay beyond the cliff to the south. The western coast would be the most sensible place to get an idea of just how dangerous Greece might have become. She beached her boat and selected a few cooking vessels for her peddler's pack; the rest she hid in a pine grove.

The first sight of the main harbor signaled things were not as they should be. Gulls sailed over calm blue waters; cormorants dove for fish; the barrier islands protecting the bay from the sea stretched rocky and bare. But the shore was empty: not a single galley beached, not a single crewman stuffing flax into seams. Set back from the harbor, up on the hill where the city should have commanded the entire coast, Pylos might as well have been Troy. Occasional smoke spirals merged with the morning haze; the city was rubble.

Marpessa picked her way through what was left of the main gates. Two half-grown women challenged her.

"Hey! What business do you think you have in Pylos?" called one.

"Whatever you're looking for's gone," laughed her partner. "If you know what's good for you, you'll find another city to visit." The women stood shoulder to shoulder, cocky grins on their faces. They whispered behind hands as Marpessa approached.

"I'm looking for a donkey." She tried out her new male voice. "I've got a sturdy fishing boat over in Ox-Belly Bay. I've got Sicilian pots, bronze-forged. You can kick them down a hill, and they won't break." She opened her pack just enough to let the sun burnish the lip of a pitcher.

Other women joined the duo. One edged closer and reached to run a finger around the rim of the pitcher. "Better than trying to find a whole one here," she muttered. "You want a donkey, you say?"

Marpessa stared at the woman. Something in the set of the brows, the long nose was familiar. A skipvine turned in her mind, a child lifting a foot. She curled her tongue around speech she hadn't spoken in years. "Are you Trojan?"

The woman stepped back, her mouth an O. "My mother was," she said slowly in Greek, "but I can't speak like that. Who're you? I never heard a man speak Trojan."

Marpessa looked around. A small crowd had gathered, all women. Their dresses were torn, their faces streaked with soot. Here and there behind a skirt, a child's face peeked out. "First, let me ask you: Pylos has been sacked, I can see. Are you all who are left in the city?"

"And we're doing just fine, thank you." A grey-head stepped out of the crowd and planted herself, hands on hips, in front of Marpessa. "Our masters ran away, brave men all. The city is ours now. We'll let you in to trade your wares, but once we've bartered, you can be off. Call this city rubble, we call it a city of women. You may have learned a little Trojan on your travels, and bronze pots might come in handy for us, but beards we don't need."

This woman's face, too, had the familiar Trojan nose. Marpessa hesitated only a moment; then she pulled the beard from her face and held out her arms.

Pylos had been attacked, she was told, not from the sea as the king and his followers had expected, but from the mountains. The first assault had caught the castle guards watching the wrong way. By the time the royal army had wheeled about, the brigands were back in the forest. The army followed them, but long spears and chariots were designed for broad plains; arrows and daggers drove them back. The see-saw between forest and citadel continued for months. On each foray, another section of the city went up in flames. When the fluted palace columns tumbled and Poseidon's wooden temple burned, the king and his followers fled in the ships they had readied against the imagined enemy from the sea. They took the royal ladies, but left most of the slaves. The brigands invited the women into the mountains, to cook for them and tend their wounded. Some went; others decided to keep the burnt city.

Marpessa listened to the story at a broken hearth in the palace. Heroes of a thousand tales had given a thousand kings pleasure in this room; on the half-fallen walls, she could see remnants of those tales—the prancing hooves of horses, the greaved knees of warriors. One wall still stood, its battle scenes whitewashed. While the singer of tales (recently a carder) drew the battle that gave them the city, an artist (recently a cook) dipped a reed first in ash, then in a bowl of blood mixed with seaweed, and sketched. By the time the tale was finished, the wall boasted three women, larger than life, brandishing swords. In front of the women, tiny ships scurried like mice across blue waves; behind, tiny horses disappeared into mountains.

Marpessa took time to teach the women the art of sailing and the skill of the bow and arrow, but when the chamomile began to flower, she was ready to continue her journey. She left Pylos with a string of mules, a pair of horses, and a dozen drovers. Some of the women thought they might make their way back to Troy to live their remaining years in their homeland; others wanted to join the Amazons. They loaded the mules with bags of gold earrings, ivory seals, bronze cauldrons, and silver cups. They ignored the chariot wheels—the new Pylians would need them for carts—and the body shields that would make solid doors, but helped themselves to spear-heads and axes and boar's tusk helmets. They left behind a city of mud-brick houses set haphazardly among the ruins. The new Pylians would survive on gatherings from the sea and the forest.

The mule train found a pass through the mountains to the farther province where farmers traded food for knives and axes. "It takes ten years to turn a battlefield back into a wheat field," a tiller told them. "In the mean-time, we scavenge the forest for what grows without plows and what falls into our hands."

Beyond the province, a gorge let them cut through another range of mountains. The brigands they met there were eager for spearheads and especially admired the Sicilian dirks. A scout helped them skirt the battle-ground where the last of the Spartans were trying to accomplish what the Pylians had not.

The road from Sparta to Mycenae was littered with broken chariot wheels and dead horses. The fleet was gone from the Argolian Gulf, carrying, Marpessa supposed, more royal families to the safety of Cyprus or

Sicily or wherever the brigands weren't. Mycenaean walls still stood, but the villages around were abandoned. From a vantage point in the shadows of the mountains, the travelers watched bronze-shielded horsemen thunder through the lion-gates with the morning sun and limp home at sunset. Whispered passwords yielded safe passage from one brigand camp to another until they reached the plains of Attica. There they found the Athenians huddled behind their walls, waiting.

The peddler band waxed as it traveled. Women who admired the brigands' lean brown bellies soon found their own bellies swelling. The lean brown brigands melted into the forests, and the mule train slowed for birthings. Strange faces appeared suddenly at evening campfires, women who had fled a mill or a farmer's field, who had heard a whisper about women traveling north to a life without masters. Often they brought their children with them.

Marpessa fretted. She had imagined a journey alone, slipping quickly through the countryside, a donkey for companion. Instead, she was a leader of women bursting with the energy of new freedom. "Why do you play with him?" she scolded a girl barely older than Lampeto had been when she'd last seen her. "He'll plant his seed and disappear. How will you climb mountains with a baby on your back?" But the women believed they could do anything, that nothing could stop them, that Marpessa would find the way for them. She grimaced and shouldered the burden.

For small feet, mountain passes seemed as high as the mountains themselves, dusty plains stretched forever, rivers were wide and menacing. Marpessa dug into her store of patience and traded wares. No matter how slowly they traveled, she counselled herself, eventually one mountain would melt into one plain that would carry them like a river to the welcoming Blackfog Sea.

Three winters found them camped in one abandoned village or another, but eventually her counsel was true: a thick, black mist rolling over a grassland was the harbinger; a wind smelling of seawater urged them on until at last, they could plunge into the sea and splash away dust and sweat and frustration. On the road north again, following the rim of the Blackfog Sea, Marpessa began counting rivers. The first forked into three mouths like a dragon; the second flowed into brackish water with stinking black mud and biting flies. The third and the fourth rivermouths formed a luminous blue lake, but as they trudged around it, the north wind silenced the water, turning it to ice. They had one last winter to wait before riding into their land of hope.

They camped outside a bustling city filled with merchants and caravans, bawling cattle and magnificent red horses. Marpessa donned her beard and went into the city to spend long evenings at an inn drinking the local mare's-milk grog and listening to tales of the steppe.

When she returned, she found women impatient for journey's end.

"Did you find out where they are?"

"Has anybody seen them?"

Marpessa ignored the hubbub and warmed her hands at the fire. She accepted a meager drumstick from a youngster and settled herself onto a log. A body pressed against her. "I hope you've got good news," the woman whispered. "The chickens stopped laying, so we've been killing them one by one. You're eating the last. No one's seen a hare for weeks, and our barley stores have weevils. The storms go on for days, and as soon as one's finished another begins. You see this log you're sitting on? There're two more underneath it. The snow piles up, and we add logs. We're southerners, you know. We're not used to this bitter cold."

Marpessa washed down her last chew with a gulp of bearberry tea and wiped her mouth. Around the fire, three dozen eager faces watched her. Even huddled together under skins, the women were shivering. She listened for a moment to the quiet of the night air: a mule uselessly pawing at packed snow; the snort of a horse. Overhead, clouds held the invisible moon hostage. She heaved a sigh.

"I was gone too long, I know. But they speak a strange tongue; I had to sharpen my ears before I could make sense of them. Yes, they know about the Amazons. They call them 'man-killers' and amuse themselves telling stories about them. They say Amazons share their grub with gorgons. They say they kill their sons, or maim them and keep them as slaves. They even say they cut off a breast the better to draw a bow. I listened for a kernel in their imaginings."

"Did you find it?"

"Did they tell you where they are?"

"Ah, where they are. That's another story. Their favorite tale is about how the Amazons appeared out of a lake and stole horses from a Scythian wagon train. The way the story goes, the Scythians chase them, but the Amazons always escape. Finally they capture one and, wonder of wonders–this is how they tell it–it is a woman. They decide they want to marry these women to bring proud blood into the tribe, so they send their handsomest young men to woo them but the Amazons won't let them approach. One lad, cleverer than the rest, sneaks up on an Amazon bathing. The Amazon, or so they tell it, doesn't send him packing, and they end up playing. Eventually all the young men are invited to a mating. The men want to marry, and the Amazons tell them to go home and get dowries. Having had a taste, the men are eager for the union, and they leave their families and bring all the horses and gold they own."

Marpessa wet her throat with tea and looked down at her hands on her knees. "And then?" echoed around the circle.

"Ah, 'and then.' I heard the story several times and each 'and then' was different. Some say the Amazons killed the men and disappeared with the horses and gold. Others say the Amazons and the men rode off together to a territory farther north or east, depending on who was telling. One man said the Amazons followed the young men back to their city on wheels, but when he told it, everyone laughed, and I heard no one else tell that ending."

"City on wheels?" someone asked. "What do you mean, city on wheels?"

"This steppe we're looking for doesn't hold deep-rooted plants; the Scythians drive cattle from one pasture to another. Some take their herds as far as the uttermost bourne where there's gold, they say, guarded by griffins.

The Scythians trade their cattle with the one-eyed men who dig it.

"As for the cities on wheels, families travel together, and their caravans make ours look like a child's toy. A family might drive fifty or even sixty wagons, each tall as a house. I found a trader who's heading south in the spring; he'll give us ten wagons for our mules. One merchant is eager for our Greek jewelry. I've already picked out some horses. We won't be a city on wheels, but we'll be a village."

"How soon do we leave?"

"How far do we have to go?"

And the child who gave her the drumstick: "When do I get to be an Amazon?"

With all the hard traveling you've done, thought Marpessa, you're an Amazon now. "We'll leave as soon as the ice breaks. The mother willing, we'll find them and our home soon." She didn't say that in all she'd heard, no one had mentioned a city where Amazons lived. If what the people at the inn said was true, there were no cities that didn't roll with the seasons. Whether the Amazons had ridden farther north to a more hospitable land or whether they, too, lived in a city on wheels, she could not guess. Their only way was to travel the great caravan route and watch and listen.

RETURN

a plain in Thrace
thirty-five years after the fall of Troy
an old woman finds her daughter

"Is this the way to Olbia?"

Ten women looked up from their noonday tea. A boy, all bone, straddled a piebald mare, his feet nearly dragging the dust. His eyes were almost hidden under tangled straw hair. The piebald stamped and snorted.

"It's the way, son," called one of the women, "but noontime's hot for traveling. Stop and give your horse a drink. Join us for tea." She pointed to a bank of trampled arbutus. Up and down the riverfront, a dozen hobbled horses snatched grass by the roots.

The boy slid to the ground and whacked his mare's flank. "Go on, girl." She shook her head and trotted down the bank. He pushed his hair from his eyes and turned to the campfire. "Thanks to you, sirs—" his jaw dropped; he stepped closer and peered at one face and then another "—uh, excuse…uh…you're all women!" He shuffled his bare feet.

"Sit anyway, son; the brew's the same no matter who

pours it. Put your name into the circle, so we may know you."

The boy's shyness faded. "Kotys. I am Kotys. My village is over there, behind that mountain, four days with my mare. With your horses—" his eyes rested on a roan as he estimated the distance from her withers to the ground "—with your horses, probably only three. I'm on my way to Olbia to find a ship to sign on as an oarsman. My back's strong; I can pull a rutting ram off a ewe... uh...excuse my mouth, I meant...."

The oldest of the women—white braids wrapped around her head, face harrowed like a field—leaned back against a poplar and closed her eyes. A chattering magpie, she thought, to amuse the others while I sleep through the day's heat. Perhaps we should camp the night here. The river's a cool place. The plain beyond stretches around a thousand poplar groves before folding itself into mountains. And then the straits, and then, only then, will the plains of Troy open to us. And open what to us? A city of shacks thrown onto a royal foundation? Pirates hoarding gold? Foreigners who claim the city? What an idea, to return to Troy. Yet if Troy took the same path as Pylos, where better to end my days? Scythian winters freeze my bones; I long to see a black-crested gull take flight from the reeds, a crane wing home in the spring.

"...well, I was betrothed to an Amazon, but she wouldn't have me. Well, she liked me, I know, but she didn't want to marry, she said, so she ran away, and I thought, if *she* could, then I would."

Marpessa sat up, eyes wide. "Say that again!" she commanded.

The boy swiveled to stare at her. "If she could, I would?"

"Before that! You were betrothed to...?"

"Oh. Her name was Iphito. We knew each other secretly before the betrothal. She used to walk with me to the pastureland."

"Not her name! Her tribe!"

"Her tribe? She was one of us. Our village is Mandra. It's on a river, too, smaller than...."

"Stop your tongue and answer me: did you call her an Amazon?"

Kotys ran both hands through his hair. He frowned at the fire and then squared his shoulders. "We call her Amazon because her mother...no, her grandmother is Amazon. She told me this, and others know it, too. Well, I guess if her granny's an Amazon, then so's her mother, but she never called her that. Only her granny. Some of the boys said it wasn't true because...." His voice trailed away under Marpessa's glare.

"Tell me her mother's name."

"Her mother is called Alexa—Alexi's wife. I don't know her childname."

Marpessa grunted. Thracian women are no better than Greek women, she thought, trading their name for marriage. Aloud, "Her granny's name, then? Or is her granny married, too?"

"Oh, no, her granny lives alone. On a mountain above the village. But her name...?" He shrugged. "I only know her as Granny. Everyone who knows her calls her that. Others call her the Amazon...or the crazy one."

Marpessa heaved herself to her feet and brushed dust from her shirt. She looked across the river to the plain that led to Troy, then back at the low mountain behind which lay a village with an Amazon. "Take me there," she said to Kotys. The other women looked at each other. "Take me," she repeated, "and I'll trade you that roan you admire for your miserable piebald." She looked around the circle of questioning faces. "You don't need me to get to Troy. I'll draw you a map. The worst of our journey's done. Or you can wait here. If I don't find what I'm looking for, I'll be back in a week. If I stay there, this boy will tell you that." She turned to Kotys who stood open-mouthed, his forgotten cup spilling tea down his legging. "You'll take me for the roan?"

"I will, sir…uh, sorry, ma'am. Do you want to go now?"

Quince trees lined the road into Mandra. Marpessa followed Kotys past fields where men struggled to steady ox-drawn plows while boys piled uprooted rocks onto a zigzag of walls. Along a wide river, women and girls pounded laundry on a row of flat rocks. In the village, under a plane tree, old men sat on stone benches, their hands thrashing in argument. One dirt street lined with stone houses led to another. Kotys finally pushed open the gate of a courtyard shaded by a tree full of ripe apples. Skeins of drying red yarn decorated the house roof. A lanky hound, stretched under the tree, barely lifted its head to greet them.

Marpessa searched the face of the woman who answered Kotys' call, looking for a sign of the sunny child she'd left on the road outside of Mycenae. What she saw were eyes narrowed against fate, a jaw set for hard times. Lampeto was slow to recognize her childname. When her eyes finally acknowledged its meaning, she shook her head in confusion. "Lampeto," she echoed, "Lampeto." She rubbed her fist back and forth along her brow.

Marpessa held out the roan's reins to Kotys. "Tell them to travel to Troy alone." Kotys whistled softly, then turned the mare and led her back the way they had come. Marpessa watched Lampeto shaking her head. "Invite me inside," she said and waited for the cloud over her daughter's face to clear.

Lampeto fanned the fire and set a clay pot over it. Her motions were abrupt, as if each action had nothing to do with the previous one. She reached down from the rafter a bunch of dried herbs, smelled them, set them aside, reached for another. Finally she dropped a handful of bayberry into the bubbling water and stared at the leaves gathering in the center of the pot. She jerked herself away from the fire and disappeared into a cloth-draped doorway. Only then did Marpessa notice the limp.

Marpessa closed her eyes and let the brew tease her nostrils. In her mind she saw herself, red-braided and young, one of three traveling over a morning road. She watched her horse stop suddenly, the others pull up beside her. She heard the voices rise and fall, but she could not quite hear the speech. A soft "He'll wither if he's too soon weaned!" floated on the bayberry steam, circled her head, and wisped into her ears. Horse and rider turned one way, then another. The second rider turned with the first, around and around, both circling the third. "Remember me!" Marpessa clutched her heart and opened her eyes.

Her daughter stood in front of her, a cup of tea in her hand. Marpessa fumbled the cup, the tea splattered, the fire hissed. Lampeto stooped to dust the ashes from the cup, then ladled it full again. Marpessa took it with both hands this time and held it to her chest. She realized neither she nor Lampeto had spoken since she'd asked to come inside. Her tongue felt thick and clumsy.

It was Lampeto finally who spoke, her voice rasping, a wind uprooting a tree. "What am I to call you?" Marpessa stared into her cup. "What am I to call you?" Lampeto repeated. "I can't call you 'Mama'; you stopped being that on the road from Mycenae."

"Marpessa, then." Short of breath, Marpessa forced her tongue to speak. "Or 'old woman', as children call me. My hair's white; I'm old." She pressed the hot cup to her lips and let the tea drizzle onto her tongue. It warmed a trail from her mouth to her belly. It's still my turn to speak, she thought, but she waited until her heart found a steadier beat. "Well, daughter…if I may call you daughter…or Lampeto. Don't make me call you Alexa. Well, then. Anger has been with you these years. Rightly, I suppose. I cut you deep. Myself, too." She looked through the open door into the back courtyard where hens scratched. She sipped tea. She pushed herself on. "I've lived these years my heart torn in pieces. I was your mother, Melanippe's kin-kith. I would be angry, too, but who dares be angry with the fates? What I did, I did." She looked at Lampeto bent over, poking the fire. "If I had the choice today, I don't know. All that I've learned since then doesn't tell me which way to turn the horse. But I know this: this split heart has never mended. I call on the mother every day to keep you in her care. Can you forgive the turning back?"

Lampeto poked her stick into the coals. She hummed a piece of a tune, then chanted: "'One fate holds the distaff, the other eyes the thread; the third, the littlest one, cuts it with a knife.' You sang me that before I could walk. Fates, yes; who can be angry with them? But they let you choose your path; I was the one left alone."

"Without me, Lampeto, but not alone. Melanippe loved you."

"Melanippe loved me," the voice mocked, "yet I live out my life here, neither in the land where I was born nor the land you promised me." She pushed her stick into the fire. A tiny flame curled out of the coals and licked it.

Marpessa shifted her weight on her stool. "You have a story to tell," she said. "I beg you to tell it."

The flame flared and consumed the stick. Lampeto limped into the back courtyard where the chickens scratched and returned with an armload of wood and two dead hens. She dumped the wood next to the fire and threw the chickens at Marpessa's feet. "When the apple tree in the front courtyard swallows its shadow, the men will come through that door wanting dinner. Build up the fire and help me pluck these birds. The bread needs another rising before it bakes. You want your story. I'll tell you."

"You see how I walk. My leg's been that way almost since you left me. While you were cuddling my brother, I was fighting off a brigand who was tired of poking ewes. Your kin-kith was fighting another. We'd have gotten away if all their valiant brothers hadn't joined the fun. When the dust cleared, my leg was smashed; Melanippe's eye was swollen shut. They took everything we had, even the horses."

Lampeto ripped the wing feathers from one of the

chickens and almost tore off the wing itself. Marpessa winced and kept her silence.

"Well, then, we had to keep moving, never mind a smashed leg and a broken eye. What one brigand gang could do, another could as well. The eye healed, but not the leg." She laughed—a sharp laugh, a laugh that could cut through bone. "We dug roots by day, ran by moonlight. Before winter set in, I was swelling. She tried to cut the baby out of me, but a brigand's seed is strong. She birthed me on the trail. At a village halfway up a mountain we begged a roof for the winter."

The chickens plucked, Marpessa singed the pinfeathers over the fire. She slit the flesh of one of them with her knife and reached in for the slippery innards. Lampeto set a three-footed pot onto the fire and filled it with water. "Onion and garlic are over your head," she said, pointing to the rafters. She pounded the bread dough on the table.

"Well, then. After the winter we got as far as this village, me dragging my leg and hefting a baby on my back. I was tired. The baby was coughing. His bottom wouldn't stop running. I was cleaning it in the river when a villager came along with a son born the same day as mine, hers twice as big and rosy-cheeked and walking already. She invited me into her home to let my baby heal. I told Melanippe to leave me, I'd go no farther, not even if a thousand Amazons were waiting."

The stew began to bubble. Marpessa searched the rafters for thyme. Lampeto set three round loaves on the hearth-ledge and covered them with a clay oven-lid. "Throw the innards to the chickens," she told her. "The feathers go into that sack over there. You can help me sweep the front courtyard. The men are leaving the fields now, and my daughters-in-law will be here with the laundry." She handed Marpessa a stick broom, and both ducked out through the door and bent to the task.

"You have your story. I stayed here while your kin-kith rode on. The mother became my sister-in-law; she lives in the house across the way. My first son got healthy, and my second was born, and then a girl, two more boys, and another girl. They're all grown. The youngest ran away this vintage. Too good to marry, that one; she listened to too many Amazon tales. Thinks she'll find them when her granny couldn't."

"Granny...you mean, Melanippe? She came back?"

"Don't be insulted, everyone calls her Granny. Yes, she came back. She traveled all of Scythia, she said, and the Amazons were always just over the hill, two mountains away, a day's journey into the sun. Wiped themselves off the earth's face, is what I say. Gone, like my childhood." She threw her broom to the side of the yard. "I can hear the men coming! Leave the broom! Get the bread before it burns!"

As she set the fresh loaves on the table, Marpessa glanced through the open door and saw a group of men passing by, young ones with mattocks on their shoulders, old ones arguing with their hands. Four turned into the courtyard. The hound that had not moved a muscle with the sweeping lumbered to his feet and wagged his tail. As the men ducked into the house, two women hurried in through the back courtyard with laundry bundles on their heads, small children trailing behind them. Marpessa folded her hands and waited to be greeted.

"Well, stranger, how do you find our village?" Lampeto's husband wiped his bowl with a crust of bread and let the hound, which had inched close to the table, lick it out of his hand. "A river that brings us sweet water, quince trees, apples and pears. The land's rich here. Stony, but rich. The wheat grows high, the tomatoes grow red, the melons sweet. The gods are good to us." He reached for an apple on the sill. "Share this with me? No?" He carved off a piece with his knife and bit it, continuing to talk through the crunches. "You traveled from the sea, you say. You didn't see a girl dressed up like an Amazon, did you?" He turned to Lampeto. "Any news of the little mosquito?" He turned back to Marpessa. "She's got to marry, you know. A woman can't be alone in this world. I let her listen to those tales her granny told her. I thought they were harmless. Amazons! Who's ever seen one in this day and age? They're all dead except for Granny." He stretched his arms over his head. "The stones were stubborn today. Tore my shirt, you can see. Sew it while I'm sleeping, will you, Wife?"

He pulled the tunic over his head and tossed it to Lampeto. The other men got up, too, and all of them climbed into the sleeping loft. The daughters-in-law tucked the children onto a feather pillow in the corner and went into the back courtyard to spread the laundry on a bush. Lampeto set the bowls down for the dog to lick and brushed the bread crumbs off the table. She handed Marpessa a potful of dried lentils. "Come on, then. We'll sit in the front courtyard. You can sort the beans while I stitch this."

The shadow under the apple tree grew until it splashed against the courtyard wall while Marpessa yearned for speech to disperse the cloud between them. Nothing came to her, and silence stretched with the shadow. Without a bridge, she thought, a chasm can't be crossed. And a bridge can't be built in a day. In the meantime, there's the other piece of my heart to gather. She shifted the kettle of beans from her lap to a stone ledge on the front of the house. Her bones were tired, but surely not too tired to climb a small mountain. Half moon tonight. If the path's well worn, I'll have no trouble. "Point me the way..." was almost on her lips when Lampeto let go the speech she had longed to hear.

"I want to call you 'Mama',"—she twisted the thread and bit it—"but it still scorches my tongue. Go to your Melanippe. The mountain path starts just across the river. When you come back...who knows? The river will still be flowing but the water won't be the same." A boy leading a goat came around the corner. "Hey, there," she called to him, "be a good boy. Take this woman to the mountain path. Lead her horse and make sure she doesn't slip on the rocks crossing the river."

Marpessa threw her pack over the piebald's saddle. Her hands hung at her side; her fingers twitched. "I'll be back," she said as she let herself out through the gate. She thought she heard a soft, "Go to the good," but it might have been the wind brushing an apple.

IPHITO

Earth shakes.
The child emerges Amazon.
She journeys out.

An Amazon Fledged

the mountain in Thrace
an old woman dying
a child going out

My second winter on the mountain was even colder than the first, but Granny's life thread remained unbroken. What songs she sang us, though, were short, sometimes no more than the color of the dawn and the sound of a horse flying over. I'd sing each fragment until my ear told me my sounds were close to hers, then carve the words into my clay tablets.

As the sun rolled away from solstice, I welcomed the lengthening days and prayed to the mother to keep Granny's breath going into the spring. Some late afternoons I'd be hurrying to complete my round of chores before night shadowed the ridge, and the wind would blow warm for a moment, tease my senses into believing spring had come up from the valley at last. Then the sun would play hide-and-seek with a snow cloud, and I'd still be pitching stable droppings onto a frozen midden.

The colt and filly had grown into a fine pair of

yearlings. The colt's grey coat had darkened till it mirrored the sky just before a storm. He ran like the wind, but his sister ran faster. She had the same flame-red coat she'd been dropped with, and whenever the sun poked its head around a cloud, she shone like my mother's copper kettle after a hard rub. I'd named her Flame and her brother Smoke.

I'd been working them since summer, and they could walk, trot, or canter to a snap of my fingers, although sometimes they still laid back their ears and laughed at me. I longed to leap on the filly and race through the woods, but I stuck to the old woman's piebald. Light as I was, I knew riding too soon could injure her. I worked them and dreamed of the day when I'd ride one and lead the other off on my own Amazon journey.

The old woman had put the idea of travel into my head. "You can't live your life on a mountain," she'd said. "Go out into the world; go be an Amazon."

She'd been with us more than a year and still she puzzled me. Every time I thought I'd got her stories pieced together, she'd tell another, and I'd have to figure how to fit it with the others. It had taken me a long time to understand that she—not Granny—was my mother's mother. Granny, then, wasn't my granny at all, and what did that make me? Was I Trojan? But I'd never been to Troy. But if I was anyway, could I be an Amazon, too? The old woman called herself Amazon, and she was born in Troy. But then she had gone to Themiscyra and kin-kithed with Granny who *was* an Amazon. But the Amazons didn't live in Themiscyra anymore, and no one knew where they did live. The old woman told stories about Scythia and cities on wheels; she talked about women she lived with on the wormwood plains who rode horses and hunted hares and fought lions and defended their wheeled city with flaming arrows. Were they Amazons? She never called them that, but they sounded like the women in Granny's songs.

I was musing on this one morning, mending a tear in the skin flap that covered the stable door when the old woman's cry pierced my puzzling.

"Iphito!"

I looked up, startled. The old woman called again, and I heard urgency in her voice. I stuck my needle into the doorpost and ran to the cave.

She was cradling Granny's head, stroking her brow. Granny's eyes were closed, and her mouth hung half-open, drool on her chin. Her breath came hard, and with each gasp her chest heaved.

"Her thread is breaking," the old woman said. "It's time to begin our goodbyes."

I stared at her and then at Granny, whose body trembled like a winter beechleaf. "No," I whispered, "not yet, Granny!" I struggled for my own breath.

The old woman nodded me closer. "Sit, Iphito. She may be with us for hours or even days, but I don't think she'll open her eyes again. She can hear you; speak to her so she can carry you with her on her journey."

I knelt and took one of Granny's feet between my hands. Even through the wool stocking, it felt like ice. I began rubbing, trying to think how to tell her what I wanted her to carry into the netherworld. I looked at the cave walls where the hearthfire danced shadows over my markings. There was burning Troy and the Trojans and the Greeks and the Amazons who died; next to the doorway to the back room, Themiscyra with horses and goats and Granny's kin all the way back to Thetis who foaled the first Melanippe. On the wall behind me were the names of the old woman's Trojan family and her royal family and her Greek family. The cities she'd lived in and the cities she'd traveled through on her journey to find the Amazons spread up to the smoke hole in the ceiling.

Behind the storage jars, a dozen clay tablets held pieces of Granny's songs. Once I'd showed her the clay markings, and she'd laughed and gurgled speech I couldn't understand. With Granny's foot in my hands, I heard the old woman say, "Use your voice," and suddenly knew what Granny had said about my tablets: Why mark songs when you have a voice?

Well, I loved making marks, but what eyes cannot see, ears may hear. I'd sung Granny's songs to the horses often enough; it was time to sing them to her. Granny could take my singing with her to the other world and know she would live in this one so long as I had breath. I would sing to my children and their children the way she sang to me, so that they would carry her beyond my breath. I opened my mouth and began.

I sang, and I found myself in another world. When I sang to the horses, I always tried to sing exactly the way Granny sang, like making marks with my voice, each mark just so and not to be changed. But when I did that, I was so busy fixing the marks, I could never remember the whole. It was the same with the tablets: each held a beginning or sometimes a piece from the middle that I remembered. But it took so long to write the marks, the rest of the song would vanish.

That afternoon, while Granny lay in the old woman's arms, peaceful as if sleeping, yet I knew she wasn't, I sang to her. I found myself forgetting the voicemarks, just singing the stories. Granny opened her good eye once, long enough to tell me she heard. I knew I sounded more like her that afternoon than I ever had in the stable.

Finally, she slept. The old woman laid her head onto a pillow and beckoned me outside.

"It's spring in the valley," she said. "Stay this night

and then leave us. Melanippe and I need this time to be together. When she's gone, I need to mourn her alone. Your task is to find others to sing your songs to. Take the mare back to your father and make your peace with your family. Ride my piebald until your yearlings have passed one more winter. I have Melanippe's old mare; that's all I'll need on this mountain."

"You'll stay here after Granny dies?"

"I have bridges to build, child."

"But where am I to go?" Water welled behind my eyes, and my knees wobbled like a newborn foal's. "You never told me where the Amazons live now. How can I find them?"

A new moon lay on its back above the ridge on the other side of the valley. So close to it they almost touched, the two brightest stars glowed steady and strong. We stood shoulder to shoulder and watched the sky grey to charcoal.

When the old woman spoke, a question came out of her mouth. "What is an Amazon?"

I sniveled. "Granny said they were…."

She cut me off. "What do you think?"

"Well, Amazons ride horses and hunt for their food and build their own houses and leave a place when it's time to go to another and aren't afraid of any man and…." I searched my mind for more.

"Where will you find such women?"

"Well, you were with women like that in Scythia and some women you traveled with went on to Troy and some you left back in Pylos and…."

"And others, it's been said, traveled south to Libya and others north beyond the steppes; others went east to the uttermost bourne and others west to where the ocean river falls off the earth. Well, then, where are the Amazons?"

I stared at the moon; it had moved up from the rim of the hills, leaving the two bright stars behind. "Everywhere," I whispered,"Amazons are everywhere."

"Then you can find them,"—the old woman squeezed my shoulder—"and you can ride with them and hunt with them and sing your songs with them. You can live without men—or you can find men who will live with you the way you live with women. Have children of your own or not; there will always be children to sing to. Wherever you go, leave marks, so that anyone who passes a thousand years from now will see what they cannot hear from your mouth."

She ducked into the cave. I heard her murmuring to Granny, her voice like a goose nuzzling goslings. I hunched under the elm and stared at the night sky. The air grew sharp with cold, and I hugged my shoulders, wishing for my cape but not wanting to go into the cave, not wanting to disturb their time together. Granny was dying, and it was time for me to leave this mountain. The old woman—and I knew I would always call her that; it fit her like a crown—the old woman said her heart lay in pieces. Maybe a heart is like an onion, I thought, one that you peel layer by layer and you cry when you leave bits with the people you love.

I rested my head on my knees and would have wept except something nudged my shoulder. It was the filly; I'd forgotten to bed down the horses. She nipped my arm. "You want your barley mash, do you?" I said, tears running down my face. She wrinkled her nose and nickered. I wanted to laugh at her funny face, but the tears kept coming, and the sound in my mouth was neither crying nor laughter, yet both.

I headed for the stable where the colt and the piebald and the old mare were waiting, the filly at my heels. I herded them all inside and filled the trough. The kingfisher, wing lopsided, scolded from her perch in the eaves, then hopped down and squeezed in for her share.

I lifted the saddlebags from the peg on the wall and began to fill them with barley. While my hands dipped, my eyes saw Granny: Granny on her black mare coming down the mountain, Granny chanting the rhythm of the stars, Granny tapping her cane and singing her song. I saw her and I sang to her:

I sing of my Amazon sisters riding flame-red horses
over dragon-plowed steppes and trembling mountain crests.
A hoof strikes rock and sends sparks:
the mother tongue rings in a thousand ears.

Photo by Stephanie Smith

Ellen Frye's connection to Greece began when she lived there in the early 1960s. Her collection of Greek folk songs, *The Marble Threshing Floor,* was published in the American Folklore Society Memoir by the University of Texas Press (1972). She is also the author of the novel, *The Other Sappho* (Firebrand Books, 1989). She makes her home in Vermont.